Myla couldn't let herself become too dependent on this man's kindness.

Nick felt her tense up, heard the defeat in her soft sigh. Cupping his hands on her shoulders, he stared down at her. "You don't have to doubt me, Myla. I want to help you through this."

She touched his face with her hand, hope warring with despair in her mind. "I know you do. And you can, with your money, with your connections, but don't you see—that's the kind of help Sonny provided. He took care of me materially, but he was never there with me spiritually. I won't be a burden to anyone again. And I won't commit to anyone who can't go the distance with me. Right now, I'm still too battered to take things any further, Nick."

Nick stood there holding her, wondering if he, too, was afraid to take things any further. But from the moment he'd looked into those luminous gray eyes, he'd been hopelessly lost. Or maybe hopelessly found.

LENORA WORTH

has written more than forty books for three different publishers. Her career with Love Inspired Books spans close to fifteen years. In February 2011 her Love Inspired Suspense novel *Body of Evidence* made the *New York Times* bestseller list. Her very first Love Inspired title, *The Wedding Quilt,* won *Affaire de Coeur*'s Best Inspirational for 1997, and *Logan's Child* won an *RT Book Reviews* Best Love Inspired for 1998. With millions of books in print, Lenora continues to write for the Love Inspired and Love Inspired Suspense lines. Lenora also wrote a weekly opinion column for the local paper and worked freelance for years with a local magazine. She has now turned to full-time fiction writing and enjoying adventures with her retired husband, Don. Married for thirty-six years, they have two grown children. Lenora enjoys writing, reading and shopping…especially shoe shopping.

I'll Be Home for Christmas

New York Times Bestselling Author

Lenora Worth

Recycling programs
for this product may
not exist in your area.

™ LOVE INSPIRED BOOKS

ISBN-13: 978-0-373-78864-4

I'll Be Home for Christmas

www.Harlequin.com

Printed in U.S.A.

And now abide faith, hope, love, these three;
but the greatest of these is love.
—*1 Corinthians* 13:13

To Jean Price and Dee Pace,
for taking a chance on me,
and
to my mother, Myla Brinson Humphries,
who's in heaven with the angels.

Chapter One

He was tired.

He was hungry.

He wanted a big roast beef sandwich from that roast Henny had baked early in the week, and then he wanted to go to bed and sleep for at least fourteen hours.

Nick Rudolph shifted against the supple leather seat of his Jaguar sedan, his impatient foot pressing the accelerator further toward Shreveport, Louisiana, the interstate's slippery surface spewing icy rain out around the sleek black car.

He was also late. Very late. Carolyn would be fuming; he'd have to smooth things over with her. Right about now, he was supposed to be escorting her to the mayor's Christmas party. Instead, he was making his way along a treacherous stretch of icy road, on the coldest night of the year.

His mind went back to the meetings in Dallas he'd had to endure to cut another deal for Rudolph Oil. After all the hours of endless negotiations, he still wasn't sure if he'd closed the deal. They wanted to think about it some more.

That he wasn't coming home victorious grated against his ego like the ice grating against his windshield wipers. Over the last few years, work had always come first with Nick Rudolph. It was an unspoken promise to his late father, a man Nick hadn't understood until after his death. Now, because he'd seen a side of his father that still left him unsettled, Nick preferred to concentrate on tangible endeavors, like making money.

Nick Rudolph wasn't used to losing. He'd been blessed with a good life, with all the comforts of old money, and he didn't take kindly to being shut out. He'd win them over; he always did. He might have given up every ounce of his self-worth, but he wasn't about to let go of his net worth.

As the car neared the exit for Kelly's Truck Stop, he allowed himself a moment to relax. Almost home. Soon, he'd be sitting by his fire, the cold December rain held at bay outside the sturdy walls of his Georgian-style mansion. Soon.

Nick looked up just in time to see the dark shapes moving in front of his car, his headlights flashing across the darting figures rushing out onto the road in front of him.

Automatically slamming on his brakes, he held the leather-covered steering wheel with tight fingers. His mind screamed an alert warning as the car barely missed hitting a small figure standing in the rain before it skidded to a groaning halt.

"What in the world!" Nick cut the engine to a fast stop, then hopped out of the car, his mind still reeling with the sure knowledge that he'd almost hit a child. Coming around the car, his expensive loafers crunching against patches of ice, he looked down at the three people huddled together on the side of the interstate. Tired and shaken, he squinted against the beam of his car's headlights.

The sight he saw made him sag with relief. He hadn't hit anyone. Immediately following the relief came a strong curiosity. Why would anyone be standing in the middle of the interstate on a night like this?

The woman stood tall, her chin lifted in proud defiance, her long hair flowing out in the icy wind, her hands pulled tight against the shoulders of the two freezing children cloistered against the protection of her worn wool jacket.

The two children, a small boy and a taller, skinny girl, looked up at Nick with wide, frightened eyes, their lips trembling, whether from fear or cold, he couldn't be sure.

He inched closer to the haphazard trio. "Are you people all right?"

The woman pushed thick dark hair away from her face, shifting slightly to see Nick better. "We're all okay. I'm sorry. We were trying to cross over to the truck stop. We…you…I didn't realize how fast you were going."

Nick let out a long, shuddering sigh, small aftershocks rippling through his body. "I almost hit you!"

The woman stiffened. "I said we're all okay." Then as if realizing the harshness of her words, she repeated, "I'm sorry."

Something in her tone caught at Nick, holding him. It was as if she'd had a lot of experience saying those words.

"Me, too," he said by way of his own apology. He'd never been good with "I'm sorry", because he'd never felt the need to apologize for his actions. But he had been driving way too fast for these icy roads. What if he'd hit that little boy?

He ran his hand through his damp dark hair, then shoved both hands into the deep pockets of his wool trench coat. "Where…where's your car? Do you need a ride?"

The woman moved her head slightly, motioning toward the west. "We broke down back there. We were headed to the truck stop for help."

"I'll drop you off," Nick offered, eager to get on his way. Turning, he headed back to his car. When the woman didn't immediately follow, he whirled, his eyes centering on her. "I said I'd give you a lift."

"We don't know you," she reasoned. "It's not that far. We can walk."

"And risk getting hit again?" Regretting his brusque tone, Nick stepped closer to her, the cold rain chilling him to his bones. "Look, I'm perfectly safe. I'll take you to the truck stop. Maybe they can call a wrecker for your car."

"I can't afford a wrecker," the woman said, almost to herself.

"We're broke," the little boy supplied, his eyes big and solemn, their depths aged beyond his five or so years.

"Patrick, please hush," the woman said gently, holding him tight against her jeans-clad leg. Gazing up at Nick, she shot him that proud look again. "I'd appreciate a ride, mister."

"It's Nick," he supplied. "Nick Rudolph. I live in Shreveport." As he talked, he guided them toward his car, wondering where they were from and where they were headed, and why they'd broken down on such an awful night. "I'm on my way back from Dallas," he explained, opening doors and moving his briefcase and clothes bag out of the way.

"We used to live near Dallas," the little boy said as he scooted onto the beige-colored leather seat. "Wow! This is a really cool car, ain't it, Mom?"

"It's *isn't,*" his sister corrected, her voice sounding hoarse and weak.

The boy gave her an exaggerated shrug.

Nick stepped aside as the woman slid into the front seat. Her eyes lifted to Nick's, and from the overhead light, he got his first really good glimpse of her.

And lost his sense of control in the process.

Green eyes, forest green, evergreen, shined underneath arched brows that dared him to question her. An angular face, almost gaunt in its slenderness, a long nose over a wide, full mouth. Her lips were chapped; she nibbled at the corner of her bottom lip. But she tossed back her long auburn hair like a queen, looking regal in spite of her threadbare, scrappy clothes.

Nick lost track of time as he stared down at her, then catching himself, he shut the door firmly, his body cold from the December wind blowing across the roadway. Running around the car, he hurried inside, closing the nasty night out with a slam.

"Mom?" the little boy said again, "don't you like Nick's car?"

"It's very nice," the woman replied, her eyes sliding over the car's interior. "And it's Mr. Rudolph, Patrick. Remember your manners."

The expensive sedan cranked on cue, and Nick pulled it back onto the highway, careful of the slippery road. "What's your name?" he asked the woman beside him.

"Myla." She let one slender hand rest on the dashboard for support as the car moved along. "Myla Howell." Nodding toward the back of the car, she added, "And these are my children, Patrick and Jessica."

The little girl started coughing, the hacking sounds ragged and raspy. "Mama, I'm thirsty," she croaked.

"They'll have drinks at the truck stop," Nick said, concern filtering through his need to get on home.

"We don't got no money for drinks," Patrick piped up, leaning forward toward Nick.

"Patrick!" Myla whirled around, her green eyes flashing. "Honey, sit back and be quiet." Her tone going from stern to gentle, she added, "Jesse, we'll get a drink of water in the bathroom, okay?"

Nick pulled the car into the busy truck stop, deciding he couldn't leave them stranded here, cold and hungry. He'd at least feed them before he figured out what to do about their car. Turning to Myla, he asked, "Is everything all right? Can I call somebody for you? A relative maybe?"

She looked straight ahead, watching as a fancy eighteen-wheeler groaned its way toward the highway. "We don't have any relatives here." A telling silence filled the car. Outside, the icy rain picked up, turning into full-fledged sleet.

"Where were you headed?" Nick knew he was past late, and that he probably wasn't going anywhere soon.

"To Shreveport." Myla sat still, looking straight ahead.

"Mom's found a job," Patrick explained, eager to fill Nick in on the details. "And she said we'll probably find a place to live soon—it'd sure beat the car—"

"Patrick!" Myla turned then, her gaze slamming into Nick's, a full load of pain mixed with the pride he saw so clearly through the fluorescent glow of the truck stop's blinding lights.

His mouth dropping open, Nick gave her an incredulous look. "What's going on here?"

"Nothing." Her chin lifted a notch. "Thank you for the ride, Mr. Rudolph. We'll be fine now."

The car door clicked open, but Nick's hand shot out, grabbing her arm. "Hey, wait!"

Her gaze lifted from his hand on her arm to the urgent expression on his face. "Let me go."

"I can't do that." Nick surprised himself more than he surprised her. "If you don't have any place to go—"

"It's not your problem," she interrupted. "If I can just make it into town, I've got a good chance of still getting the job I called about yesterday. Once I find steady work, we'll be fine."

"I can help," he said, almost afraid of the worn wisdom he read in her eyes. "I can call a wrecker, at least. And find a place for you to stay."

From the back seat, Jessica went into another fit of coughing, the hacking sound reminding Nick of memories he'd tried to suppress for too long.

"That does it." He reached across Myla to slam her door shut. The action brought them face-to-face for a split second, but it was long enough for Nick to get lost in those beautiful eyes again, long enough for him to forget his regrets and his promises and wish for things he knew he'd never have. And it was long enough for him to make a decision that he somehow knew was about to change his life. "You're coming with me," he said, his tone firm. "I won't leave a sick child out in this mess!"

The woman looked over at him, her eyes pooling into two misty depths. "I...I don't know how to thank you."

Nick heard the catch in her throat, knew she was on the verge of tears. The thought of those beautiful eyes crying tore through him, but he told himself he'd only help the family find a safe place to spend the night. He wasn't ready to get any further involved in whatever problems they were having.

"You need help," he said. "If you're worried about going off with a stranger, I'll call someone to verify my identity." A new thought calculating in his taxed brain, he added, "In fact, my sister is a volunteer counselor for Magnolia House. I'll call her. She's always helping people." Having found a way to get out of this sticky predicament, Nick breathed a sigh of relief.

Myla turned back, her eyes wary. "What's Magnolia House?"

He waved a hand. "It's this place downtown, a homeless shelter, but a bit nicer. According to my sister it has private rooms where families can stay until...until they get back on their feet." He really didn't know that much about his sister's latest mission project, except that he'd written a huge check to help fund it.

Giving him a hopeful look, she asked, "And we don't have to pay to live there?"

"No, not with money. You do assigned tasks

at the home, and attend classes to help you find work, things like that. My sister helped set the place up and she's on the board of directors. She'll explain how it works."

"Can you get us in tonight?"

Putting all thoughts of a roast beef sandwich or a quiet evening with Carolyn out of his mind, Nick nodded hesitantly. "I'll do my best. And I'll send a wrecker for your car, too."

She relaxed, letting out a long breath. Then she gave him a direct, studying stare, as if she were trying to decide whether to trust him or not. Clearing her throat, she said, "Thank you."

Admiration surfaced in the murky depths of Nick's impassive soul. He knew how much pride those two words had cost this woman. He admired pride. It had certainly sustained him all these years. Debating his next question, he decided there was no way to dance around this situation. Starting the car again, he carefully maneuvered through the truck stop traffic.

"How'd you wind up…?"

"Homeless, living in my car?"

Her directness surprised him, but then this whole night has been full of surprises.

"If you don't mind talking about it."

"My husband died about a year ago." She hesitated, then added, "Afterward, I found out we didn't have any money left. No insurance, no savings, nothing. I lost everything."

Nick glanced over at her as the car cruised farther up the interstate, leaving downtown Shreveport at Line Avenue to head for the secluded privacy of the historic Highland District. Taking her quiet reluctance as a sign of mourning, he cleared his throat slightly, unable to sympathize with her need to mourn; he'd never quite learned how himself. So instead, he concentrated on the fact that she was a single mother. All his protective instincts, something he usually reserved for his sister, surfaced, surprising him. *Must be the Christmas spirit. Could I possibly have some redeemable qualities left after all?*

"What did you do?" he asked, mystified.

Lifting her head, Myla sighed. "I left Dallas and looked for work. I got a job in Marshall, but the company I worked for closed down. I ran out of money, so we got evicted from our apartment."

Nick could hear the shame in her voice.

"After that, we just drove around. I looked for work. We stayed in hotels until the little bit of cash I had ran out. That was two weeks ago. We've been sleeping in the car, stopping at rest areas to bathe and eat. The kids played or slept while I called about jobs."

She slumped down in her seat, the defeat cov-

ering her body like the cold, hard sleet covering
the road.

Then she lifted her head and her shoulders.
"I don't want to resort to going on welfare, but
I'll do it for my children. We might be destitute
right now, but this is only temporary. I intend to
find work as soon as I can."

It was Nick's turn to feel ashamed. He was
more than willing to write her a fat check, but he
had the funny feeling she'd throw it back in his
face. She had enough pride to choke a horse, but
how long could she survive on pride? And why
should he be so worried that she'd try?

Nick didn't have time to ponder that question.
Minutes later, he pulled the car up a winding
drive to a redbrick Georgian-style mansion that
shimmered and sparkled with all the connota-
tions of a Norman Rockwell Christmas. Suddenly, the wreaths and candles in the massive
windows seemed garish and mocking. He'd told
Henny not to put out any Christmas decorations,
anyway. Obviously, the elderly housekeeper
hadn't listened to him, not that she ever did.

Now, seeing his opulent home through the
eyes of a person who didn't have a home scared
him silly, and caused him to take a good, long
hard look at his life-style.

"Man!" Patrick jumped up to lean forward.

Straining at his seat belt, he tugged his sleeping sister up. "Look, Jesse. Can you believe this? Santa's sure to find us here. Mr. Nick, you must be the richest man in the world."

The woman sitting next to him lowered her head, but she didn't reprimand her son. Nick saw the pain shattering her face like fragments of ice.

Nick Rudolph, the man some called ruthless and relentless, sat silently looking up at the house he'd lived in all his life. He'd always taken it for granted, his way of life. His parents had provided him and Lydia with the best. And even in death, they'd bequeathed an affluent life-style to their children.

Nick had accepted the life-style, but he hadn't accepted the obligations and expectations his stern father had pressed on him. When he could no longer live up to those expectations, he'd acted like a rebel without a cause—until he'd seen the truth in his dying father's eyes.

Everything his father had drilled into him had become a sham. And Joseph, overcome with emotion because he loved his Ruthie too much, had tried to tell Nick it was okay to be vulnerable when it involved someone you loved.

But it had been too late for Nick. He'd learned his lessons well. Now, he guarded his heart much in the same way he watched over Rudolph Oil—

with a steely determination that allowed no room for weakness.

Maybe that was why he'd felt so restless lately. Maybe his guilt was starting to wear thin. Though he had it all, something was missing still. Nick had never wanted for anything, until now. All his money couldn't buy back this woman's pride or settle her losses. All his wealth seemed a dishonest display compared to her honest humility.

"No, Patrick," he began, his voice strangely husky, "I'm not the richest man in the world, not by a long shot."

"Well, you ain't hurtin' any," Patrick noted.

"No, I suppose I'm not," Nick replied, his eyes seeking those of the woman beside him. "Let's go inside where it's warm."

Opening the car door, he vented his frustration on the expensive machine. He *was* hurting. And he didn't understand why. How had the night become a study in contradiction and longing? How had he fallen into such a blue mood? Well, he'd just had an incredibly bad day, that was all. Or was it?

No. It was her—Myla. Myla Howell and her two needy children. He couldn't solve all the problems of the world, could he? He'd make sure they had a decent place to stay, maybe help her find a job, then go on with his merry life. Things would go back to the way they'd been up until about an hour ago.

And how were things before, Nick? an inner voice questioned.

Normal. Settled. Content.

And lonely.

And that was the gist of the matter.

These three ragamuffins had brought out the loneliness he'd tried to hide for so long. Denying it had been pretty easy up until tonight. But they'd sprung a trap for him, an innocent but clever trap. They'd nabbed him with their earnest needs and unfortunate situation. He'd help them, sure. He certainly wasn't a coldhearted man.

But he wouldn't get involved. At all. His formidable father had drilled the rules of business into Nick—no distractions, show no emotions. In the end, however, Joseph Rudolph had forgotten all his own rules. In the end, his own emotions had taken control of his life. Nick had learned from Joseph's mistake. So now, he let Lydia do the good deeds while he took care of business. It was a nice setup. One he didn't intend to change.

"I'll call Lydia. She'll know what to do," Nick said minutes later as he flipped on lights and guided them through the house from the three-car garage. A large, well-lit kitchen greeted them as the buzz of the automatic garage door opener shut them snugly in for the night. Nick headed to the cordless phone, intent on finding his sister fast. Then he'd have to call Carolyn and make his excuses. When he only connected with Lydia's perky answering machine, he left a brief, panicked message. "Lydia, it's your brother. Call me—soon. I'm at home and I could really use your help."

We make him uncomfortable, Myla Howell reasoned as she watched the handsome, well-dressed man talking on the phone. She knew she and her children were an inconvenience. When you didn't have money, or a place to sleep, you became that way.

She'd learned that lesson over the last few months. People who'd called themselves her friends had suddenly turned away. She wasn't good enough for them now. They didn't have time for her now. They couldn't be seen associating with a homeless person.

This man was the same. He couldn't wait to be rid of them. But, he had saved them tonight. She'd give him credit for that. She watched him moving about the kitchen, taking in his dark, chocolate-colored hair, remembering his gold-tinged tiger eyes. Golden brown, but missing that spark of warmth. Calculating eyes? She'd seen that kind of eyes before; still bore the scars from trusting someone who could be so ruthless. Would this man be any different?

She hoped so, she prayed so, for the sake of getting her children to a safe place. Refusing to give in to her fears or her humiliation, she focused on her surroundings instead. What a joy it would be to cook in a kitchen like this! She missed having a kitchen. Cooking was one of her pleasures and with hard work and lots of prayer, it could soon be her livelihood, too.

The gleaming industrial-size aluminum stove shouted at her while the matching refrigerator-freezer told her there was lots of bounty here to explore. The long butcher block island centered in the middle of the wide room spoke of fresh vegetables and homemade breads and pastries. Myla closed her eyes briefly, almost smelling the aroma of a lovely, home-cooked holiday meal. She'd miss that this Christmas. But next year…

Nick watched her in amazement. Under the surreal lights of the truck stop, she'd looked pale and drawn. But here in the bright track lights, Myla seemed to glow. She was tall, almost gaunt in her thinness. Her hair was long and thick, a mass of red, endearing curls that clung to her neck and shoulders. Even in her plain clothes, this woman exuded a grace and charm that few women would possess dressed in furs and diamonds. Obviously, she hadn't always been homeless. Her clothes and the children's looked to be of good quality and in fair shape. Not too threadbare; wrinkled, but clean.

Mentally shaking himself out of his curious stupor, Nick watched her closely, noticing the dreamy expression falling across her freckled face. Then it hit him. "You're probably hungry."

His statement changed Myla's dreamy expression to a blushing halt. "I'm sorry…this is such a beautiful kitchen…I got carried away looking at it." Nodding at the expectant faces of her children, she pushed them forward. "The children need something to eat. We had breakfast at a rest stop—donuts and milk."

The implication that they hadn't eaten since this morning caused Nick to lift his head, but he turned away before she could see the sympathy in his eyes. "Well, don't worry. Our housekeeper, Henrietta Clark, has been with the family for most of my life. She always stays with a friend down the street when I'm away, so she's not here tonight. But she cooks a lot, way too much for my sister and me. We usually wind up giving half of it away—"

"It's all right, Mr. Rudolph," Myla said to ease his discomfort. "We'll be glad to take some of your leftovers off your hands, right, kids?"

She was being cheerful for the children's sake, Nick realized. Relaxing a little, he dashed over to the gleaming refrigerator. "Let's just see what we've got. We'll have ourselves a feast."

Patrick hopped up on a wooden stool, yanking his fleece jacket off with a flourish. "My mom's the best cook, Mr. Nick. She can make just about anything, but her bestest is bread—and cookies."

"Oh, really?" Nick glanced over at Myla. "Well, come on over here, Mom. I could use an expert hand. I'm not very good in the kitchen."

Eyeing Jesse and unsure what to do with her, he lifted the quiet little girl up on the stool next to Patrick. With an unsteady smile, he registered that she felt warm, almost too warm, but then he wasn't a doctor or a daddy. What did he know about little girls?

Myla stepped forward, then took off her threadbare wool coat. "Anything I can do to help?"

Nick watched as she hovered beside him, as if waiting for him to issue an order. Tired and unsure what to do himself, he unceremoniously loosened the red-patterned tie at his neck, then yanked off the tailored wool suit jacket he'd worn all day. Tossing the jacket across a chair, he watched as Myla straightened it and hung it over the back of the chair, her hands automatically smoothing the wrinkles out.

"Thank you," he said.

He watched as a flush bathed her cheeks. "I'm

sorry," she said. "Force of habit. My husband liked everything in its place."

Nick nodded, then wondered about her marriage. Had it been a happy one? Not that it was any of his business, but the sad, almost evasive look in her eyes made him curious. Did she miss her husband? Of course, she probably did, especially now when she was struggling so much.

"How about a roast beef sandwich?" he asked as he lifted the heavy pan of meat out of the refrigerator. "Henny cooked this for Sunday supper, but I didn't get back into town to enjoy it."

"That's a shame."

"No, that's the life of an oilman. Lots of trips, lots of leftovers." Searching through a drawer, he found a large carving knife. "I say, let's cut into this thing."

"Yeah, let's cut into that thing," Patrick echoed, clapping his hands. "My mouth's watering."

Jesse smiled, then coughed.

"Are you hungry, Jesse?" Worry darkened Myla's eyes. "She has allergies and she's fighting a nasty cold."

A spark of warmth curled in Nick's heart. "Maybe some good food will perk her up." He offered Jesse a glass of orange juice.

Nick found the bread, then poured huge glasses of milk for the children. Myla located the coffeemaker and started a fresh brew. She sliced tomato and lettuce, then made some thick roast beef sandwiches. Soon all four of them were sitting around the butcher block counter. Nick picked up his sandwich for a hefty bite, but held it in midair as Myla and her children clasped hands and bowed their heads.

Seeing his openmouthed pose, Myla said quietly, "We always say grace before our meals. I hope you don't mind."

Nick dropped his sandwich as if it were on fire. "No, of course not."

When Myla extended her hand to his, something went all soft and quiet in his ninety-mile-an-hour mind. When was the last time he'd said a prayer of any kind? He listened now to Myla's soft, caressing voice.

"Thank you, Lord, for this day and this food. Thank you for our safety and for the warmth you have provided. Thank you for sending us help when we needed it most. We ask that you bless each of us, and this house. Amen."

Stunned, Nick wasn't so sure he wanted his house blessed. He felt awkward as he lifted his hand away from the warmth of Myla's. To hide his discomfort, he said, "Let's eat."

Patrick didn't have to be told twice. He attacked one half of his sandwich with gusto. Nick flipped on a nearby television to entertain the children, but mostly to stifle the awkward tension permeating the room.

He watched them eat, hoping Lydia would call soon. Patrick wolfed his food down in record time, while Jesse nibbled at hers between fits of dry coughing. Their mother broke off little bits of her sandwich, as if forcing herself to eat, her eyes darting here and there in worry.

Finally, out of frustration more than anything else, Nick said, "That hit the spot. I was starved."

"Me, too," Jesse said, speaking up at last.

Nick's eyes met her mother's over her head. It didn't help to know that Jesse probably had been really hungry, when to Nick the words were just a figure of speech. Myla only gave him a blank stare, though, so to hide his confusion he munched on a chocolate chip cookie while he watched the children, and their mother when she wasn't looking.

The baggy teal sweater brought out the green in her expressive eyes. Worn jeans tugged over scuffed red Roper boots encased her slim hips and long legs. Couldn't be more than thirty, just a few years younger than him, yet she carried a lot of responsibility on her slim shoulders.

"You've got a pretty name," he said to stop the flow of his own erratic thoughts.

"I was named after my grandmother," she said. "She hated her name because people would always call her Mi-lee. My mother named me after her to make her feel better about it."

"Where's your family?" he asked, hoping to learn more about her situation.

She shot him that luminous stare before answering. "My parents passed away several years ago—a year and a half apart. First my mother, from a stroke. Then Daddy. The doctors said his heart gave out, and I think that's true. He died of loneliness. They'd been married forty years."

Nick felt a coldness in the center of his heart, a coldness that reminded him of his firm commitment to keep that part of himself closed away. "Same with my parents. My mother died of cancer, and my father was never really the same after her death." He looked down at his half-eaten sandwich. "He…he depended on his Ruthie, and her death destroyed him. It was as if he changed right before my eyes." Not wanting to reveal more, he asked her, "Do you have any brothers or sisters?"

She nodded. "A brother in Texas—he's got five kids. And a sister in Georgia. She just got married a few months ago." She sat silent for a minute, then finished. "They don't need me and my problems right now."

"Do they know…about what's happened to you?"

Her flushed face gave him his answer. She

jumped up to clean away their dishes. "No, they don't. Not yet." Turning toward the sink, she added, "I really appreciate your help, but I don't intend to live on handouts. If my job hunt pays off—"

"What sort of work are you looking for?"

"A waitress, maybe, for now. I love to cook. One day, I'd like to run my own restaurant."

Nick wanted to touch her face for some strange reason. She had that dreamy look about her again, and it endeared her to him. He felt an overwhelming need to buy a building and turn it into a restaurant.

But he didn't touch her, and he didn't offer to fund her venture. Instead, he looked down, as embarrassed by being wealthy as she obviously was by being destitute.

Myla's touch on his arm brought his head up. "I want to thank you, Mr. Rudolph, for helping us. All day, I prayed for help, and then you came along. You offered us shelter, and that's something I'll never forget. So thank you, for your kindness and your understanding."

Nick looked in her eyes and felt himself falling, falling, as if in slow motion. Moving away abruptly, he said, "Call me Nick, please. And you don't have to thank me."

The confused look she gave him only added to his woes. He couldn't tell her that he rarely let people get close enough to touch him, either physically or emotionally. He couldn't erase the hurt look in her eyes.

When a special news bulletin interrupted the noisy cartoon on the nearby television, Nick was thankful for the distraction until he heard the report.

The familiar face of the local weatherman filled the screen, and after going over the progress of the ice storm covering the city, the newscaster suggested everyone stay put for the night. "The roads are becoming treacherous and travel may be hazardous until this storm passes. We should be able to resume normal activities by midmorning when higher temperatures and sunshine clear this system out."

Nick eyed the television, willing the man to say it wasn't so. When that didn't happen, he looked toward the silent phone, all hopes of Lydia's much-needed help freezing up like his winding driveway outside. With three pairs of questioning eyes centered on him, he could only give a gracious but shaky smile.

Thoroughly at odds, he wanted to ask Myla Howell why him? Why'd she have to pick him? And what was he supposed to do with her now? Instead, he took her hand. "Well, that settles it. You heard the man. You can stay here tonight."

"What?" Myla gave him a stunned look. "But

what about your sister? What about Magnolia House?"

"It can wait," Nick stated firmly, silently wishing Lydia would call and rescue him before he drowned in those questioning green eyes. Or was he silently hoping she wouldn't call? To counter his treacherous thoughts, he added, "It's late and Magnolia House is downtown. It's too dangerous a trip in these icy roads. You'll have to stay here tonight."

"Are you sure?"

"Very sure." His tone was firmer than his confidence. Right now, he wasn't very sure of anything—except that he couldn't send this family back out into that cold, dark night.

Chapter Two

"Henrietta, please don't cry."

Nick ran a hand through his tousled hair, then gratefully accepted the cup of coffee the whimpering housekeeper handed him before she burst into tears again.

"Ah, Henny, don't do that. It's too early in the morning for theatrics. I didn't know my Christmas present would move you to tears."

"But, Nicky," the older woman began, her shimmering gray curls not moving a centimeter even though she bobbed her head with each word, "it's the sweetest thing anyone's ever done for me. God bless you. You're a good man…a good one…" Her words trailed off as her watery eyes centered on something beyond Nick's head.

Nick turned to find Myla Howell standing in the doorway, wearing the same clothes she'd had on the night before.

"I'm sorry," Myla said, sensing she'd interrupted something important. "I heard voices...."

"Nicky?"

Myla looked from the old woman who stood with her hands on her hips to the man sitting like a king at the head of the long Queen Anne dining table. He was trying to read the newspaper, and judging from the frown marring his handsome face, he was losing patience with the woman standing before him.

"Who's this?" the woman asked, smiling kindly over at Myla.

Nick looked up. Myla didn't miss the surprise or the grimace on his face. "Oh, hello. Henny, this is Myla Howell. Due to the bad weather, Myla and her children were forced to spend the night in one of the guest rooms." He extended a hand toward the woman. "Myla, this is Henrietta Clark, my housekeeper and best friend."

Myla was thankful when the woman didn't ask any questions. "Nice to meet you."

Henny smiled and waved a hand. "Did I wake you up with my wailing, honey? I'm sorry, but I'm so excited. Nicky gave me the best Christmas present before he left for Dallas the other day—a trip to see my daughter and her children in Arkansas."

"And she's wailing because she's so touched," Nick added on a droll note. "She's leaving today."

"That's wonderful," Myla said. "I know you'll have a great time."

"I plan to," Henrietta said, "if I don't spend the whole time worrying about Nicky and Lydia."

"We'll be fine," Nick said, his attention already back on his paper. Then he asked Myla, "Would you like some breakfast, a cup of coffee, maybe?"

Myla took the cup of coffee Henny pressed into her hand, but she didn't sit down. "Actually, I came down to ask for some medicine. Jesse's had a bad night. She's running a fever."

Nick scowled. "Is she all right?"

Afraid that he wasn't pleased at this added problem, Myla nodded. "I think she'll be okay. I just need to bring her fever down."

"Your child?" Henny asked.

"Yes. My oldest. I'm not sure about her temperature, but she feels awfully hot."

Henny whirled around. "There's a thermometer around here somewhere. Nicky won't let me use it on him anymore."

A smile slipped across Myla's face. In spite of her concern for Jesse, she couldn't resist the mental image of the stout Henrietta chasing a snarling Nick around with a thermometer.

Nick's scowl went a few grooves deeper. "She still thinks of Lydia and me as her babies." He gestured for Myla to sit down. "Does Jesse need anything else?"

Myla appreciated the warmth in his words, even if it didn't quite reach his eyes. "I don't think so. Just rest and good food. If you don't mind, I'll feed them breakfast before we leave."

He looked down at the table. "I put in another call to my sister. You can't take chances with this weather."

"No, I wouldn't do that to Jesse. I appreciate your letting us stay here, Mr. Rudolph."

"Call me Nick."

"Okay." Myla sensed, knew, he couldn't wait to be rid of them. "I'm sorry we've disrupted your life."

"It's no problem," he said. "Did you sleep all right?"

"Yes, we all did until Jesse started coughing."

Myla wouldn't tell him that she'd tossed and turned in spite of the warm, cozy room and the enormous bed. She felt so alone, so out of place in this grand old house. But she was certainly thankful that they hadn't had to spend the night in the car.

When she looked up, Nick's gaze softened. "Don't worry about your daughter. If she's sick, we'll get her to a doctor."

"Thank you."

Henrietta burst through the swinging door

from the kitchen, a bottle of pills in one hand and a thermometer in the other. "How old's the child?"

"Eight."

"Half a tablet, then. And I'll fix her up some of my special hot lemonade with honey to help get that down. The lemons—good for a cold." She turned to strut back to the kitchen, then whirled to face Nick. "Oh, Nicky, I almost forgot. Are you sure you and Lydia can handle things tonight?"

Nick looked confused, his gaze moving from Myla to his housekeeper. "Tonight? What's going on tonight?"

"Your dinner party," Henny said with arms akimbo. "Don't tell me you forgot to call the temp service. You told me not to worry about a thing, that you and Lydia would take care of calling someone to fill in for me."

Nick sat up, realization hitting him. "You mean my sister and I are in charge of…kitchen duty?"

Henrietta shook her head. "I knew you weren't listening to me the other day." She shot Myla a knowing look. "A one-track mind, that one. If it don't have to do with oil, he don't want to deal with it."

"I guess I *wasn't* listening," Nick agreed. "And I think we'd better round up someone to take care of that. We both know Lydia's as useless in the kitchen as I am."

The housekeeper mumbled something about preoccupied executives, then explained, "It's too late to call the temp service. They're booked through Christmas, I imagine." Looking disappointed, she asked, "You want me to stay?"

Myla listened, then squeaked, "I can do it." When both Nick and Henrietta looked at her as if she'd gone daft, she wanted to drop through the tapestry rug underneath her feet. But this would be a good way to pay Nick back for his help, and it would make her feel a whole lot better about things. "I can cook. I can do whatever needs to be done." When Nick kept staring at her, she rushed on. "Well, if I'm going to stay here all day anyway, I can't just sit around twiddling my thumbs. I'd like to help, to pay you back for your kindness."

Henny smiled from ear to ear. "Well, now, isn't that a nice gesture on your part, honey."

"I'll pay her, of course." Nick gave Henny a sharp look, then turned a questioning glance at Myla. "Do you have experience with this sort of thing?"

Myla didn't tell him that she'd once been considered the best hostess in her neighborhood. That had been one of her husband's demands, along with all his other demands. Instead she said, "I've been in charge of dinner parties before, yes. Henrietta can show me where everything is." Lifting her chin, she added, "And I could use the money."

She watched as Nick weighed his options, hoping for this reprieve, this time out of the cold. Finally, he spoke.

"Well, I certainly don't have time to find anybody else. Okay, you've got the job. But I expect everything to run smoothly—and that means making sure your children—"

"They'll stay out of your way," Myla said. "I promise."

"Good." He turned to Henny. "After breakfast, you can get things settled up between you."

"You're the boss," Henrietta said, smiling to herself as she ambled into the kitchen.

Nick watched her, and Myla saw the doubt clouding his features. Wanting to reassure him, she said, "Don't worry. I can do whatever needs to be done. I want to help and I won't let you down."

"That's good," he contended, "since I'm trusting you alone in my house."

Not liking his tone, she retorted, "I'm a Christian, Mr. Rudolph. I won't steal anything if that's what you're implying."

"I wasn't implying anything. And I certainly didn't mean to insult you."

Seizing the opportunity, Myla rushed on. "Then you might consider letting me fill in for Henrietta. I could work for you until she gets back from her trip."

That got his attention. "I hadn't planned on a long-term replacement. I don't go all out for the holidays."

"That's a shame," she countered. "Christmas is such a beautiful, blessed time of year."

"I don't like Christmas," he insisted. "In fact, this dinner party tonight is more of an obligation to my clients than a celebration."

"Why wouldn't you want to celebrate?" she had to wonder out loud. "The birth of the Savior is a joyous time."

He didn't give her the answer she wanted. Instead, he said, "Henny's planning to be gone until the first of the year. Are you willing to work through Christmas?"

Myla was glad, but surprised that he wanted her to stay that long. She needed a job, but hadn't counted on this becoming a long-term arrangement. This would give her some time, though, and a safe place for her children. "A month? That would help us get a good start on the new year."

Nick's next words were dusted with doubt. "And, it would solve both of our predicaments— you need a job, I need a good worker."

"What about my children? You obviously don't want them underfoot."

"We'll get them enrolled in school. You were planning on doing that, weren't you?"

Resenting his superior attitude, she retorted, "I hadn't thought past getting them to a warm bed."

Nick countered. "Hey, it was your idea. After Christmas you can take the money you've earned here and do whatever you like. This is a sensible solution for everyone concerned."

Myla had to agree. "So you're asking me to stay here and work for you for the next few weeks?"

He almost grinned. "I don't remember doing any asking, but yes, I guess I am."

She held out her hand. "Deal, unless that other job I came here for is still open. Then, I'll help you only until I can start there."

"Deal," he said, shaking her hand. "I'm glad you understand that this is only temporary."

"Oh, I understand. And I'll need to get my car. We've got a few belongings left in the trunk."

"I'll take care of that. You take care of your daughter, then get together with Henny so she can explain how everything's run around here." He started toward the long, central hallway, then turned. "We'll put you in Henny's apartment off the kitchen. It's more private."

"That's fine," Myla said. At least it would be

a roof over her head for a while, and it would be much more suitable than the spare guest room, since this was a strictly business arrangement. "I'd better get back up to the children. Jesse needs this medicine."

"Don't forget Henny's hot lemonade with honey," he reminded her. "Works wonders. I've got to get to work. Oh, and one other thing. I always do a background check on my employees. Any problem with that?"

Hesitating, Myla stammered, embarrassed. "No, but I think you should know a few things. I haven't held a job since high school. I was…I chose to stay at home after my children were born. And my credit is shot because…I had to file bankruptcy."

He gave her a sympathetic look that hid his own doubts as to the wisdom of this arrangement. "Anything else?"

"Isn't that enough?" she replied with a small smile. "I'll do a good job, I promise," she added sincerely.

Nick stared down at her a moment, nodded briefly, then turned to go.

She watched Nick walk away, then she sent up a silent prayer. *Don't let me mess this up, the way I've messed up my life.*

She'd be so ashamed if he knew the whole truth.

* * *

"This is so exciting!"

Lydia Rudolph stood at the window of her brother's downtown Shreveport office, gazing out at the Red River some twenty floors below. "I mean, I'm twenty-five years old, big brother, and this is one of the few times I've actually seen you do something almost human." She fluffed her shining blond bob and beamed brighter than the lighted Christmas stars twinkling insistently on the building across from them. "This only goes to show what I've tried to tell you all along— doing something good for someone brings out the best in people, even an old Scrooge like you."

"I am not a Scrooge," Nick said in protest. "I can't help it if I don't feel the same strong sense of religion that you do, Lydia. I'm quite happy with my life the way it is, thank you. In fact, I'm just a happy-go-lucky kind of guy."

Lydia snorted, causing her bright red hoop earrings to jingle. "Right. You're a great faker, Nick, and we both know it. But this is a start. I'm glad to see you involved with something besides this oil company."

"Yes," Nick responded dryly from his perch on the massive teakwood desk. "Having two rambunctious children and their pretty mother in my house for the holidays is about the most excit-

ing thing I can imagine. And here I was hoping
you'd help me out of this mess."

"They're people, Nick, not a mess." Lydia
swung around, the fringe on her red suede jacket
almost hitting her brother on the head. "I think
you needed this. You couldn't wait to tell me all
about it when you got here this morning."

"I told you all about it because what I need is
your help, little sister. *They* need your help. This
is a very temporary situation."

Nick wished he'd just kept his mouth shut. This
whole business was starting to get to him. Still
amazed that he'd hired Myla to run his house,
he had to wonder at his own sanity. He was reeling from the strange turn of events in his life. In
the span of less than twelve hours, he'd committed himself to saving a homeless mother and her
two waifs. Not involved? Hah! He was involved
up to his eyeballs.

Resolving to get this situation cleared up—
another of his father's rules: no loose ends—
Nick gave his sister a pleading look. "This dinner
party is important, Lydia. I need to reassure some
of our local stockholders. We've pulled through
our slump, but I've still got people jumping ship.
Are you going to help me?"

"I'm thinking," Lydia said, settling herself
down in the comfortable black leather swivel
chair behind Nick's desk. "If I help you with

this woman and her children and your precious party, will you go to church with me on Christmas Eve?"

Nick gulped his coffee too fast and burned his tongue. "That's blackmail," he said, spurting out hot coffee in the process. "You know how I feel about that."

Lydia's knowing smile didn't help his bad mood. "What happened to that almost-human I was just talking to?"

He scowled, rubbing his burned tongue against his top teeth. "I'm the same as ever. And I refuse to be pushed into a situation about which I feel uncomfortable. If you can't agree to help me, please leave. I've got work to do."

Lydia jumped up to come around the desk. "Oh, Nick, remember when we were little? Remember Mother taking us to the Christmas Eve service? You in your Christmas suit, me in my velvet dress? You cared then, Nick. You loved Christmas."

"Well, I don't love it now," he said, his mood getting darker by the minute. "And I have work to do."

Lydia stood staring at him. "And I thought helping someone out of a jam would make you less grumpy. When are you going to stop being mad at God, Nick?"

"Probably never," he said, tired of this argument. Thinking back about last night, he remembered Myla's prayer. She'd thanked God for simple things. Basic things. Things most people took for granted every day. Arrh, there he went again, daydreaming about a woman he'd just met last night. "Look, Lydia," he said, "I won't kick them out. You know that. But we do need to help them. And since this sort of thing is your department…"

Lydia nodded. "Of course I'll help. But you made the right decision, Nick. Giving her a job was the best thing you could do."

"I didn't have much choice. She was available on the spot and I needed someone immediately. Now I hope I don't live to regret it."

"You won't," Lydia assured him as she headed toward the door, her long black wool skirt swishing around her matching boots. "You did need someone immediately, and I don't think you'll regret it at all."

"Hey, you're the bleeding heart, remember?" he replied. "While you've been out trying to save the world, I've been breaking my back to save this company."

"And you've done a good job," his sister acknowledged. "The latest stock report shows we're up forty cents per share. We haven't had to dip into that old pile of money Daddy left us, so why don't you relax?"

Nick's eyes grew dark. "I promised him—"

"No, you swore on his grave," she reminded him. "Nick, when are you going to forgive and forget? Yes, he was harsh, but he was only human. It's just that we didn't see his human side until it was too late. I don't want it to be too late for you, Nick. But you're already headed down the same road he took—giving orders and doling out cash, never getting your hands dirty, never facing reality. It's not too late for you yet, not if you realize that money isn't everything."

Nick eyed his little sister curiously, still amazed that she'd escaped their father's iron-handed approach to life. Lydia was so like their mother—good, kindhearted, openly loving. And, Nick reminded himself bitterly, he was his father's son. "Look, Lydia, doling out cash is what I do best. Money, I've got."

"Uh-huh. And that's about all you've got."

Defending himself, he said, "Well, I haven't heard any complaints. We've both got everything we need."

She shook her head. "Except faith, Nick. That's the one thing I've got that you lack." With that, she shut the door and left.

She was wrong, of course. He didn't need the added assurance of some higher power watching over him, which she insisted on believing. He had everything he needed. Didn't he? Head of a successful company, owner of one of the finest homes in Shreveport, possessor of a social book that rivaled anybody's in Louisiana. His list of attributes spoke volumes about his life.

But that's about all you've got. Lydia's words taunted him again. Oh, all this Christmas sentiment was affecting his better judgement. It was normal to feel at odds with so much Christmas hype being shoved down his throat.

Remembering other, happier Christmases, Nick stared out the window, mindless of the crawling traffic below. His father had taught him to keep his emotions at bay, and had set a firm example by never showing any sort of affection or compassion himself. Until Ruth died. Watching his proud, self-sufficient father crumble had only reinforced Nick's own need to stay in control.

Now, he was trapped, so trapped, in a firmly encased persona that gave him a ruthless outlook on life. He'd get through Christmas the same way he had each year since his parents' deaths, by celebrating with a detached kind of fascination, like the cynical kid who didn't believe in Santa anymore.

Except this year, he reminded himself, he'd be doing it with a lovely widow and her two noisy kids. "Why do I have a bad feeling about this whole thing?" he asked himself.

* * *

"The whole thing is going to be a disaster," Myla mumbled to herself as she once again checked preparations for the dinner party that loomed less than two hours away. Henrietta had gone over all the details with her. The food was ready; it only needed to be heated when the guests arrived. But Myla wasn't so sure about herself.

She wore a white long-sleeved blouse and black trousers, courtesy of Lydia's closet. Henrietta had insisted Lydia wouldn't mind or even miss the functional outfit.

"All you have to do is keep the food coming," the older woman had explained. "Nicky likes everything to run smoothly—these people are clients and stockholders, but this is a casual dinner. Just put it out on the buffet, real nice and hot, and keep your eyes open for seconds. The bar's fully stocked, and Nicky'll mix what drinks are needed."

Since she didn't condone drinking, Myla was glad she didn't have to play bartender. The rest sounded simple enough. After all, she'd done this hundreds of times before. Smoothing the knot of hair coiled at the nape of her neck, she took a deep, calming breath. The children were tucked away in Henny's small sitting room, armed with books to look over, coloring pads and crayons, and various other things Henny stockpiled for her grandchildren. They could watch a little television before they were to go on to bed. Surely, nothing could go wrong.

The kitchen door swung open. Nick marched in, whistling to himself. He'd saved the Dallas deal, another coup for Rudolph Oil, and a nice nibble to share with his fidgety stockholders. Stopping in midwhistle, he looked around the kitchen, and then into the set of exotic eyes watching him.

"Who did all of this?" he asked in a deadly calm voice as his gaze trailed over the fresh ivy and holly berry greenery adorning every available corner. The scent of bayberry candles lifted through the air, giving the room a cozy holiday effect.

Seeing the scowl on his face, Myla said, "I...I did. I found the decorations in the garage. I thought it would look nice for the party."

"I don't care for a lot of frivolous decorations," he said, noting that she looked right at home. "I just wanted a simple, quiet evening with no fuss. Did the cake I ordered come?"

She nodded, swallowing back her embarrassment. "Yes, your coconut cake is right here on the counter."

So it was. To avoid lashing out at her for her

innocent assumptions, he concentrated instead on the rich cake he'd had a local restaurant prepare for tonight.

Before he could speak, she spoke to him. "I'm sorry about the decorations. I didn't realize—"

"Never mind," he said on a tired sigh. "It is Christmas, after all, and I do need to appear all jolly-holly for these people."

Myla leaned against the counter to steady her nerves. "Everything's in order. The table's set. The food's ready. I really didn't have that much to take care of."

"Plenty to drink?" he asked as he scanned the mail lying on the countertop.

She lifted her shoulders. "Yes, but I must tell you, I don't drink and I'd prefer not to have to mix drinks for your guests."

He shrugged. To each his own. "I'll take care of that, then. But don't worry. I don't expect this stoic crowd to get too wild."

Relieved to hear that, Myla relaxed a little. "Henny told me how important this is to you."

He moved into the room, throwing his briefcase on a desk in the corner before heading to the refrigerator. "Henny's very efficient. She knows how these functions work. The old-boy networking system never slows down."

Myla noticed the lines of fatigue around his eyes. He seemed so cool and in charge that she found it hard to believe he could be worried. "Can I get you anything?" she asked.

"Nah, I'll just have some juice." Spying a tray of appetizers in the refrigerator, he picked up a cracker covered with a shrimp mixture and popped it into his mouth. "That's good," he said between chews.

"I found the shrimp in the freezer," she explained. "I know the recipe by heart."

"You're in charge of the kitchen," he said by way of appreciation. "Do you need anything?"

I need to have my head examined, she thought. She was terrified of being here, but she needed this job. She wouldn't allow her children to be homeless again.

"No, Henny went over the schedule with me."

"Good." Nick placed the empty juice glass in the sink. "Guess I'll head up to get a shower." Turning back on his tasseled loafers, he asked, "How's Jesse?"

"Much better." Touched that he'd bothered to ask, Myla guessed he was just being polite. "Her fever is down." At his questioning look, she added, "They're in Henny's room, all settled in."

He nodded, wondering why he'd become so tongue-tied all of a sudden. "By the way, your car's in the auto shop. It should be fixed in a couple of days. Your belongings will be delivered tomorrow."

"But…" Myla began, not knowing how to ever thank him. He'd taken care of everything in such a businesslike manner. She supposed he was used to taking matters into his own hands, while she was just beginning to learn how to deal with everyday problems on her own. "Thank you," she said, her voice tapping down the tad of resentment she couldn't deny.

He raised a hand to ward off her gratitude. "It was no trouble and besides, I'm depending on you to run my house. You can't do that if you're out trying to get your car fixed."

"Good point," she reluctantly agreed. He didn't take compliments or praise very well. "I'm sorry for all this trouble."

Nick shrugged. "Don't worry. If it'll make you feel better, I'll send you the bill."

"I insist," she said as she watched him plow through the swinging door to the hallway. Somehow, she'd pay him back for his kindness, but she couldn't say if it would make her feel better or not.

Nick's bellowing call from the den brought her head up. Rushing through the swinging door, she flew down the hall to the other room to find him standing in front of the tree she and the children had put up that afternoon.

"What's this?" he asked, his hands on his hips,

his chin jutting out as he stared at the eight-foot-tall evergreen.

"It's a Christmas tree, of course," she said, wondering why the fresh-cut tree seemed to be bothering him so much. "Henny called a nursery and had it delivered."

Nick ran a hand through his hair and gave another long sigh. "I told her in no uncertain terms, that I did not want a tree in this house."

"She never mentioned that to me."

"No, I don't suppose she would have. Well, too late to take it down now."

Finding her courage, Myla stepped closer to the tree to touch one of the brilliant ornaments she'd found in a huge box in the garage. "The children had such a great time decorating it, I'd appreciate it if you would try to enjoy it."

Nick's gaze moved from the tree to the woman at his side. Her eyes were almost the same shade as the lush branches reaching out toward him. And they sparkled every bit as brightly. He couldn't deny her this one concession to his rigid holiday rules.

"Okay. The tree can stay up, but no more decorating without consulting me first, no matter what Henny tells you."

"All right."

He didn't like her tone or the hurt look in her eyes. "What are you thinking?"

She smiled then, but her eyes still held a certain sadness. "That you have a beautiful house. Six bedrooms, is it? And four baths? And those sunrooms. I've always loved having lots of live plants in a sunny room."

Nick hadn't really noticed the plants. He shrugged, his gaze sweeping casually over his surroundings. "It's almost too big for a bachelor and his baby sister, but it's home."

"Is it?" she couldn't help but ask.

"Is it what?"

"Home?"

"I live here, don't I?"

"Yes, but…oh, never mind. This place is like something out of a dream, but it just seems as if something is missing in this great, old house."

She'd sensed it, when she'd gone through the rooms earlier, dusting and gawking at the same time. The house was as reserved and cool as the man who lived in it, and just like him, it cast out a false sense of contentment.

Nick sighed, then turned to go. "Don't try to analyze me, Myla. There's nothing missing here. Everything is as it should be."

"If you say so."

She watched as he left the room and stalked up the curving staircase. How sad that he couldn't enjoy the holidays. Myla wondered what had made him this way. She turned back to the tree, her gaze fixed on the gold and white angel watching her from the top of the sturdy blue spruce. "I think Nick Rudolph needs your help," she whispered.

An hour later, the house was filled with the sound of laughter tinkling on the air as crystal glasses tinkled with ice. The aroma of mulling cider wafted through the night while the fire in the massive marble fireplace located across one wall of the den crackled and popped. Myla viewed the cluster of people scattered around the tree, making sure each guest had plenty to eat and drink, while she listened to the carefully selected group's conversation.

"Nick, I love the house this year," a stout woman covered in diamonds said between bites of puffed pastry stuffed with artichoke filling. "I haven't seen it this festive and bright in a long time."

Nick's smile was all calculated charm. "Glad you approve, Dottie. I'm not much on the holidays, but my new housekeeper insisted I put up a tree, at least." He guided Dottie away from the tree, then said, "Remind me to show you Rudolph Oil's fourth-quarter report. I'd love to have you serve on the board again. We could use your input."

Clearly enthralled, the woman practically

preened. "You know, I've been telling Jacob we need to reconsider that decision."

Jacob, a tall gray-haired man, listened diligently. "Whatever you say, dear."

Nick grinned, then caught Myla's eye. He saw the disapproving look she cast his way and wondered what he'd done to offend her. Excusing himself from Dottie, he cornered Myla by the buffet.

"Is everything all right?"

"Fine," she replied, her gaze scanning the crowd. "Would you like another glass of soda?"

He finished off the cool liquid left in the bottom of his glass, then shook his head. "No, but I'd like to know why you were glaring at me earlier."

"No reason," she said, busying herself by putting out more cans of soda for his guests. "I was just watching you work the crowd."

"And you disapprove?"

Myla gave him a direct stare. "No, I'm just surprised. One minute you're acting like a regular grizzly bear and the next you're turning on the charm."

Recalling their earlier encounter right here in this room, Nick replied, "Look, I'm sorry I got angry about the decorations and the tree. You were smart to spruce this place up...and it looks wonderful. Perfect."

"Glad you approve," she said, not at all convinced of his sincerity.

Sensing that she didn't exactly trust his motives, Nick smiled over at her. "I do approve. So far, everything's going according to schedule. And I owe that to you."

Before she could respond, he turned away to greet some more guests, leaving her with the memory of his aftershave. She'd smelled it earlier when he'd entered the kitchen. He was a handsome man. A self-reliant man, who liked to rule over his domain.

This was his world, not hers. She'd had a similar life with her husband, but now…now, she intended to make her own way, with her faith to shield and guide her. She wouldn't put her trust in another ruthless man. And Nick Rudolph was exactly that.

She watched him play host to the hilt as he mixed business with pleasure and made her feel like an out-of-place Cinderella watching the prince dance with all the other girls at the ball.

"Bill, you rascal," Nick said, laughing as he playfully slapped the tall, blond-headed man on the back. "How are things looking for your re-election to the Senate? Can I depend on you down in Baton Rouge?"

"Can I depend on your donation to my next campaign?" Bill countered with a hearty laugh, thus beginning a rather long and detailed account of his political aspirations. His wife, a slender brunette in a pricey red pantsuit gave a bored smile as her eyes fell across Myla, then moved on.

The look of dismissal galled Myla, but she knew her place. She'd been poor before she married Sonny Howell. And now, she'd come full circle. She could afford to be gracious to the woman; she'd once been so like her.

Once again, Nick excused himself from his guest to head toward Myla with a purposeful stride. Afraid that she'd done something wrong again, she moved to meet him.

"Everyone's here except—" Nick stopped in midsentence when a loud screeching noise, followed by a bellowing bark and the crash of dishes, rose from the back of the huge house. "What was that?"

The doors of the kitchen burst open as a tall woman with flowing blond hair ran into the room, her black dress clinging to her slender curves.

"Carolyn?" Nick looked surprised, then laughed in relief. "Leave it to you to make a grand entrance."

The lovely Carolyn fumed with indignation. "Nick Rudolph, how dare you laugh at me? It's bad enough that you stood me up last night, but now this. You've got to do something!"

"Do what?" Nick looked confused. "What's the matter?"

The other guests had gathered around now, each waiting and watching as Carolyn pulled at a torn spot in her black hose. "It's Pooky," she said on a low moan. "He's in the kitchen—"

Another wailing scream rose from the kitchen, followed by a growl and another scream, this one human. Several loud crashes joined in with the screams.

Nick plopped his glass down on a walnut table. "What's going on in there?"

Carolyn moaned again and tugged at her hair. "That's what I'm trying to tell you, Nick. I brought Pooky along with me to ward off muggers and when I went to put him in Henny's room, a...a cat ran out and now Pooky's chasing the crazed creature around the kitchen and when I tried to stop him, well...that cat lurched into my leg and well, look, a fifteen-dollar pair of nylons ruined." Tossing her evening bag and black velvet cape into Nick's face, she added, "And I'm bleeding. You know I'm allergic to cats!"

The uproar in the kitchen increased now, the crowd moving in closer, each guest hovering near the swinging doors, afraid to go in and see what Pooky and the mysterious cat were doing to each other.

"Cat?" Nick shook his head. "I don't have a cat."

Another scream brought Myla into action. Pushing through the dazed spectators, she called to Nick, "The children!"

"Children?" Carolyn eyed Nick suspiciously. "I thought I saw something unusual hiding behind Henny's couch. Nick, what's going on here?"

Nick looked over at Carolyn, prepared to explain everything until he heard Myla's low agony-filled moan. That moan did not bode well, not at all. Giving Carolyn's things to the skinny brunette in red, he dashed toward the kitchen. The sight that greeted him caused him to echo the same low-pitched moan.

A tabby cat, scrawny and hissing, sat on a blade of the still ceiling fan, one paw extended in the attack position while a howling, barking Saint Bernard sat underneath, his tongue fairly hanging out of his big, toothy mouth as he waited for the next chase to begin.

Patrick sat in the middle of the counter, surrounded by what had once been the carefully arranged entrees for the dinner party. Now those entrees were not only arranged all over the counter, but also all over Patrick and all over the once-white tile floor. Jesse hovered in the doorway leading to Henny's apartment, her wails matching pitch with the cat's. The Saint Bernard, tired of playing chase with the pitiful cat, turned and started lapping up what remained of the platter of roast that Myla had carved so lovingly and garnished with parsley and star-burst carved cherry tomatoes.

Myla's eyes met Nick's. Of their own accord, her hands came up to cover her face. He's going to send all of us packing, she thought.

Nick's face burned with a rage born of shock. "What happened here?" His voice grew deeper and more deadly with each word. "Would someone like to tell me what in blazes happened in here?"

The room, filled with twelve warm, curious bodies, remained silent, except for the occasional hissing from the ceiling fan and the melodious lapping on the tile floor.

"I'm waiting." Nick circled the carnage, his eyes brown with a fire of rage. "I want some answers, now!"

Finally, a feeble voice rallied from the direction of Henny's room. Jesse stepped forward, shivering with fear, her eyes bright with freshly shed tears. "Mamma, we forgot to tell you about the cat," she said before she burst into another round of high-pitched sobs.

Chapter Three

The door leading from the garage burst open. Lydia bounced into the room, wearing a black crepe dressy pantsuit, her blond bob shining as brightly as her diamond earrings.

Myla recognized her from the many pictures of Nick and Lydia hanging around the house. But Carolyn...was she Nick's girlfriend? Nick had been busy doing a good deed last night and now look what it had caused him. Even Lydia's upbeat mood didn't help the situation.

"Sorry I'm late," she began, her earrings twinkling like twin stars, "but I had to stop by—" Her eyes registered shock for a split second before she burst out in a fit of uncontrollable laughter. "Food fight? Nick, why didn't you tell me? You know how I love to throw my food at you!"

"Not now, Lydia," Nick said, his growl more pronounced than the drooling Pooky's. "We've had a bit of an accident and I was just trying to get to the bottom of it."

"Looks like Pooky here beat you to it," Lydia countered, rushing forward to pet the massive Saint Bernard. "Hey, boy, what did you get into this time?"

"It's not Pooky's fault," Carolyn said as she sidestepped a pile of shrimp dip to comfort the hyper dog. "I walked over for the party, so I brought Pooky with me. I had no idea that a cat and two strange children would attack us when we entered the back door."

"Next time, try using the front door like the other guests," Lydia replied sweetly, though her eyes indicated she felt anything but sweet.

"Ladies, please," Nick said, raking a hand through his crisp dark curls. Turning to Myla, he watched as she knelt to comfort her sobbing daughter. Instantly, he regretted his anger from before. "Jesse, how'd we manage to acquire a cat?" he asked, his tone deceptively soft, his eyes centered on Myla as if to say *this is your fault*.

Jesse looked up to her mother for reassurance. Myla, stung by Nick's anger and by Carolyn's high-handed attitude toward her children, shot him a defiant look. Thinking she could kiss this new job goodbye, she patted Jesse on the shoulder. "Just tell the truth, honey."

Jesse took a deep breath to clear away another

round of sobs. "Mr. Nick, I'm sorry. But today when Momma was getting stuff ready for your party, me and Patrick went for a walk out in the backyard. We weren't supposed to, 'cause I'm sick and Patrick gets into stuff, but we snuck out…. Anyway, we heard a cat meowing behind that big building by the pool. Patrick came back in the house when Momma wasn't looking and got some food for the cat. It was real hungry." Sniffing, she looked up at Nick. "We wanted to help it so it wouldn't freeze to death, like you helped us, Mr. Nick." She wiped her nose again with her hand, her big blue-green eyes wide with the importance of her confession.

Nick looked uncomfortable, but Myla saw the touch of warmth Jesse's innocent words had provoked in his eyes.

"Why didn't you tell me about the cat, sweetie?" she asked her daughter, her heart breaking. Jesse loved animals. She'd never let one starve or stay out in the cold, in spite of her allergies around certain animals. Hunger wasn't pretty—in animals or humans.

"We were afraid you'd make us let it go," Jesse said, dropping her eyes to the floor.

"Yeah, and we didn't want Mr. Nick to kick us out," Patrick piped up as he held out his dip-covered fingers. "I tried to catch it, Mamma, but it was too fast. And besides, I'm scared of that big dog."

"Pooky wouldn't hurt a flea," Carolyn protested, looking from one child to the other accusingly. Then she turned to glare up at Nick. "You told me you helped some people out last night; you didn't tell me they were staying in your home."

Bristling, Myla shot Carolyn a proud look. "I'm *working* for Mr. Rudolph while his housekeeper is on vacation."

"Working for Nick?" Carolyn whirled around. "Is that true—even after what you told me last night?"

Nick's look warned her to drop it. "Things have changed since then. I'll explain later."

Myla's eyes met his. He was embarrassed, but she saw the hint of an apology. He was too much of a gentleman to make a scene. Obviously though, he'd avoided telling Carolyn everything. Wondering if he was ashamed of her being here, Myla felt like a circus sideshow.

Deciding she'd really give them all something to talk about and try to save Nick's reputation and her much needed job in the process, she pinned Carolyn with a level look. "Yes, it's true. Mr. Rudolph was kind enough to help us out last night. You see, we've had a rough time lately. We've been living in our car." That statement caused an audible rumbling through the room, but it didn't stop Myla. "He found us stranded on the interstate during the ice storm, and he brought us here. Knowing I needed a job, he asked me to work for him while his regular housekeeper, Henrietta, is on vacation. And as long as he doesn't have a problem with that, I don't, either. I'm just very thankful that he was kind enough to care about my children and me.

"The Bible says, 'Blessed are ye that hunger now: for ye shall be filled. Blessed are ye that weep now: for ye shall laugh.' Yesterday, I was hungry and weeping. Today, thanks to Mr. Rudolph's kindness, I'm warm and full and laughing, in spite of all of this mess." Dismissing Carolyn's surprised, cynical look, she turned to Nick. "Isn't this the true spirit of Christmas? You took us in, when there was no room at the inn. You did something entirely unselfish. It's the best Christmas present I could ask for, and I thank you. And I take full responsibility for my children's actions."

Nick stood still, in shock. He should be angry that she'd turned his party into a sermon on the mount. Instead, he felt a great rush of warmth moving through his body. Ashamed, he blinked to hold back the blur of tears forming in his eyes. He'd never seen a woman as brave as Myla Howell. She had more courage among this crowd of cutthroats than he'd ever possessed, ruthless as he was supposed to be.

Of course, her courage was one thing. Being called a pushover was quite another. Glancing around, he waited for the looks and whispers that were sure to come. But to his surprise, his guests didn't condemn him or laugh at him. They came, one by one, to pat him on the back.

The senator was the first in line. "Perfect, my friend. Helping the homeless is one of my campaign pledges. I'll hold you up as an example."

That comment was followed by Dottie's tear-filled pledge. "How could I ever doubt your sincerity again, Nick? Jacob and I will be happy to serve on the board of Rudolph Oil, and I intend to call our broker first thing tomorrow and instruct her to buy a substantial amount of Rudolph Oil shares." Then, glancing at Myla, she whispered, "And I'll leave a check for your housekeeper, too. A little Christmas gift. Such a tragedy."

"But…" Nick didn't know what to say. Myla had single-handedly turned a disaster into a public relations dream. Now, after giving her eloquent speech, she went on to introduce herself to the group and assure them that they would have a decent meal, after all.

Sending Nick a daring look, she called, "Pizza, anyone?" Then, turning to him with a gracious smile, she whispered, "You can't fire me now."

"I wouldn't dream of it," he whispered back, his eyes full of a grudging admiration, and his heart full of something warm and unfamiliar.

All the guests started talking and laughing, except Carolyn. Myla saw the blonde throw Nick a scrutinizing look.

Carolyn stood, then smiled sweetly at Nick. "Since when did you find religion, Nicky?"

Nick didn't answer. Instead, he said, "Carolyn, why don't you wait for me in the den?"

"I'll order the pizza," Lydia said, jumping over broken dishes to find the phone. "How about three vegetarians and three with pepperoni and sausage, all large with extra cheese?"

Everyone clapped their approval. Lydia herded the humans and Pooky toward the den. "Just make yourselves at home while I dial the emergency pizza number."

Carolyn gave Myla a cold look, then pranced into the den with the rest of the crowd. As she walked past Nick, she said, "We really need to talk."

Nick watched her go, then turned to stare at his wrecked kitchen, before settling his gaze on Myla and her daughter. Lifting Patrick down, he sent the little boy scooting toward his mother. A long sigh escaped from deep within Nick's lungs as he watched Patrick hug Myla's neck and smear her with shrimp dip. How could he be mad at them when they stood huddled together as if he were about to issue an order for their execution?

"I'll clean it up immediately," Myla said, her voice firm while her hands shook. "I'm so sorry, Nick."

He held up a hand to ward off her apology. She'd put up a good front for his guests, but he could see she was visibly upset. She'd said she'd handled a few dinner parties, but never one such as this, he'd wager.

"It's okay," he said, pushing away his questions for now. Swallowing the lump of pride caught in his throat, he added, "Thanks. You sure handled that better than I did. You made me sound like a saint."

"Saint Nick," Patrick said, giggling as he wiped a glob of dip on his pajamas.

"Not a saint, Patrick," his mother corrected, "just a very kind and understanding man."

"Flattery will get you everywhere," Nick retorted, smiling in spite of himself. "You obviously have me confused with someone else."

She wouldn't let him get away so easily. "Oh, no. I know what I'm talking about. You're uncomfortable in this role, being heroic, I mean. What happened to make you so afraid of reaching out to others, Nick?"

Lydia hung up the phone, interrupting before he could answer. "I can't believe Carolyn. She knows that dog doesn't belong at a dinner party. She should have left the big brute at home to run around on that two-acre lot she calls a backyard."

"She brought him along for protection," Nick said, glad to change the subject.

Lydia snorted. "I've never know Carolyn to need protection."

"Careful, sis."

Lydia turned to Myla and the children. "He's right. I have to remember not to judge too harshly. It's so nice to meet you. Nick's told me all about you."

Myla looked at Nick. Yes, she was sure he'd called Lydia first thing this morning, telling her how much he regretted being a Good Samaritan. "Well, he apparently didn't tell *Carolyn* all about us."

Getting back to the immediate problem, Nick said, "I'm not worried about Carolyn or her dog right now." Motioning toward the fan, he said, "What about that?"

The cat still sat on guard, its bright yellow eyes narrowing suspiciously each time anyone made a move.

"We'll get it down and clean it up, don't worry," Lydia said. "How about we call it Shredder, kids?"

"Yeah, Shredder," Patrick agreed, clapping his sticky hands together.

"Who said we were going to keep it?" Nick asked, his hands on his hips.

"The worst is over." Myla turned to Lydia. "Would you mind getting Shredder out of the way so I can clean this up?"

"Sure." Lydia called softly to the frightened animal. "We'll take him to Henny's sitting room and teach him some manners while you two straighten things out." The meaningful gaze she shot her brother told him she was referring to much more than the mess on the floor.

"Gee, thanks." Nick pulled off his navy-and-burgundy patterned wool sweater, then rolled up his blue shirtsleeves so he could get down to work. "Lydia, you just want to see me get my hands dirty, right?"

Lydia bobbed her head and grinned.

Myla stepped forward as Lydia bribed the cat down with a piece of roast beef. "Nick, you don't have to help."

The animal refused to come into Lydia's arms, but did jump down and run into the safety of Henny's apartment. Lydia and the giggling children followed, discussing the now famous battle with animation.

Left alone, Nick and Myla could only stand and stare around them. Everything was ruined. Nick moaned softly when his eyes lit on the mashed remains of his prized coconut cake.

"You have guests," Myla stated, picking up the cake plate to remove the source of Nick's woes. "Go ahead. I'm sure Carolyn needs comforting after her horrid ordeal."

Nick heard the sarcasm in her words and saw the twitch of a smile pulling at her lips. He relaxed and smiled back, his eyes meeting hers. "Carolyn Parker and I grew up together," he explained. "She's divorced and rich, and expects me to jump when she calls. We escort each other around town on various occasions. And about last night—"

"You don't have to explain anything to me." Myla sidestepped a pile of spinach salad. "Your social life is your business. But why didn't you tell her everything…about me?"

"Because I didn't think I owed her an explanation. I didn't feel the need to go into detail about your situation."

"That was considerate," she said, thinking he was one of the most gentlemanly men she'd ever met. Then again, maybe he used his impeccable manners as a shield.

Nick tried to take the flattened cake from her. He wanted a little taste of that wonderful cake before she threw it out. "I'm glad you understand."

"Oh, I understand." She turned, looking for the trash can. "And I'm really sorry the children ruined your party." He tried to pry the cake out of her hand, but she pulled it away. "Nick, I've got it. Why don't you get a mop from the—"

Nick made one last-ditch effort to reach for the cake, leaning forward from the waist so he wouldn't have to step in the pile of spinach salad. But just as he lunged forward, Myla turned to dump the cake in the trash.

Nick came crashing against her, knocking Myla completely off balance. The cake sailed up as she whirled around. He got a taste of his cake, all right, in the face, as he slipped in salad dressing, with cake and Myla sliding right into his arms. By the time the impact was complete, Myla had cake all over her face and shoulders, too. Unable to move or breath, she watched as Nick licked creamy almond-colored icing off his lips.

His arms holding her, and the remains of the mushed cake, against him, he asked, "Are you all right?" When she nodded, he licked his lips again, causing something like kindling wood to spark and curl in Myla's jittery stomach. "Ah, that's so good," he said, lifting his hands to dump the ruined cake into the trash. "I could have handled anything but losing my coconut cake. I think I'm going to cry."

Myla huffed a breath, then turned to find

a towel. "Please, if you do, don't mess up the floor."

"Very funny."

Nick raised a hand to take the towel from her, his fingers gripping her wrist. Lifting her head, she saw a set of bronze-colored eyes lazily assessing her. Gone was the cold indifference, the quiet reserve, and in its place, a heated brilliance that took her breath away.

"Let me go, Nick," she said on a soft whisper.

"Wait, you have a big glob of cake on your right cheek."

Reaching up, she touched her face. "I'll get it off. Now, let me go so we can clean up this mess."

"Let's start right now."

Before she could move or protest, he began wiping her face, his fingers gently lifting icing and cake filling off her cheek, his amused gaze causing sparks to ignite again in her stomach. She tried to pull away, but he held her steady.

"Right there." He took the towel and wiped it across her jaw. "Yep, that's it." He held her away to inspect his handiwork. "All clean now."

Myla could only stare at him. What on earth was the man trying to do to her? Here she was, covered with cake and shrimp dip, in the middle of his kitchen, with her children and his sister in one room and a pack of hungry guests as well as a jealous girlfriend in the other. Everything was ruined, and Nick should be angry with her. Instead, he was treating her with such intense concern that she thought she might cry from the sheer sweetness of his gesture. She could have handled his anger; his kindness was much harder to bear.

"Are you finished?" she managed to ask as she gritted her teeth to keep the lump in her throat from choking her.

Nick, seeing the torment in her eyes, stood back, then carefully wiped bacon-and-mustard salad dressing from his khaki trousers. Thinking he'd made her uncomfortable, he said, "I'm sorry. I didn't mean to offend you, Myla."

To calm her own wayward feelings, Myla turned to the sink. "It's all right. I…I'm just surprised that you didn't…that you aren't—"

"What?" Confused, Nick tugged her around again.

Myla sighed, then took the towel from his hands. "You should be mad—I promised you everything would work out fine tonight, and now I've ruined your party. Why didn't you just get mad at me?"

A bit amused, Nick lifted a brow. "So, you're upset because I'm not upset?"

She bobbed her head. "Yes. No! I mean, I

could have handled you shouting and ranting. Why did you have to be so nice to me?"

Nick watched as she frantically tried to wipe the counter, not knowing how to comfort her. "I am so sorry," he repeated, a mock glare coloring his face. "What was I thinking?"

"Exactly," Myla agreed, unaware that he was smiling behind her back. "You don't have to be nice!"

Nick understood that she wasn't used to any tenderness and that realization bothered him. What had she suffered, to make her so wary of a kind gesture? He wanted to ask her, but decided she'd just clam up if he tried. So instead, he teased her. "I promise, if this happens again, I'll try to be justifiably angry."

She whirled around just in time to see the sparkle in his eyes. Hiding a smile, Myla relaxed a little. "Guess you miss Henny, huh?"

He laughed. "Yeah, but her dinner parties were never this exciting, I have to admit." Pivoting, he said, "I'll go get the mop."

Her hand shot out to stop him. "Wash your face first."

Lydia stuck her head around the corner from Henny's apartment. "By the way, Nick, I thought you both should know—I stopped by Magnolia House on my way over here. They're full, probably will be until well after the first of the year.

But Myla, I did put your name on the waiting list."

Myla looked up at the man who'd saved her, praying he'd let her stay until she could find somewhere else to go.

Nick didn't say anything, but she could tell by his blank expression that he wasn't too pleased with the news. Together, they silently cleaned the kitchen while Lydia got the children and Shredder off to sleep.

Finally, when they'd finished and the whole room had been restored to order, Nick turned to Myla. "Well, at least you can stay here until the first of the year."

"Yes, and I'm thankful that the good Lord led me to you."

He gave her a puzzled look, then said, "Maybe it's the other way around, Myla."

Myla's heart soared. Maybe he was beginning to feel differently about Christmas and helping others. She followed him into the den where Pooky lay fast asleep in front of the roaring fire. The guests were playing a game that involved telling the truth regarding scruples.

Carolyn turned to Nick. "Your turn, darling. Are you willing to test your scruples?"

"Scruples?" Nick laughed, his shrug indifferent. "Why, you all know I don't have any. None at all."

Myla sat watching him. He had deliberately downplayed his good side, the side she'd seen firsthand. *You're wrong, Mr. Rudolph. You have scruples—you just haven't used them in a while.*

Again, she had to wonder what had caused Nick to turn into himself. As she watched him, his eyes touched on her and she saw the warmth shining there. She said a silent prayer. *Dear Father, help Nick to find his way back to you. And thank you for leading me to him.*

The next night when Nick came home from work, he found a freshly baked pound cake sitting on the counter, its buttery aroma filling the house. The kitchen sparkled and gleamed. Holly branches from the garden decorated the counters, giving the room a homey effect.

The back door opened and Myla, Patrick and Jesse all rushed into the room, giggling and chattering. All three held arms full of firewood. Myla looked up, a hesitant smile cresting her lips.

Patrick said, "Hey, Mr. Nick. We're gonna start a fire."

"So I see."

He nodded toward the boy's mother, noticing the way the December wind had brightened her cheeks and pinkened her lips, giving her fair skin a perfect contrast to her fiery wind-tossed copper-colored hair. As was his nature, Nick watched and waited as she ordered the children to place the wood in the den.

"And don't try to light a fire. I wouldn't want you two to burn down the Christmas tree." Turning back to Nick, she said, "Dinner will be ready in an hour."

"That's fine." He gazed at the fat cake sitting on the counter. "That smells wonderful."

"Want a slice?" She headed toward the refrigerator to pull out the milk. "Milk or coffee?"

"Milk." Nick slid out of his khaki trench coat. "This looks good."

"Well, it's not coconut cake, but I wanted to make up for last night. I hate seeing grown men cry."

He chuckled, then took the glass of milk and a generous slice of the still-warm cake, his eyes following her as he bit into the flaky lemon-flavored mound. Myla waited as he chewed it with glee, a little moan of appreciation escaping as he swallowed.

"I think I'm in love," he murmured as he closed his eyes. After another hefty bite, he said, "Oh, you wouldn't believe the phone calls I've been getting all day."

Concerned, she asked, "About what?"

"About you. About the pizza party. We really impressed the stockholders. They're throwing their support toward Rudolph Oil, and you."

"Me?"

"They want to help you out."

Myla had to turn away to keep him from seeing the tears welling in her eyes. Maybe there was hope, after all. Of course, these people didn't know her background. She wondered how they'd feel about her if they knew the whole story. "I can't take any charity, Nick," she said to hide her fears.

"Of course you can," he reasoned. "They admire your strength, Myla. Last night, you showed them something they've taken for granted."

She shrugged, her back still turned away. "I only told the truth according to my beliefs. It's what I live by."

Thinking she was about to launch into another sermon, Nick cleared his throat. "I have some checks here. Will you take them? You can use the money after…after you leave here."

"Charity," she said, dreading the thought of not being self-reliant.

Nick came to stand beside her. "Yes, charity, but given with the best of intentions. And besides, they can write it off on their income tax, so take the money, Myla."

She stopped stirring the steaming pot of vegetables. "The Lord loves a cheerful giver."

"That's the spirit. You can always pay them back."

She smiled then. "Did they write checks?"

"Yes, why?"

"I'll record their names and addresses and offer them my services. I want to start my own catering business."

He stared over at her. "Catering…you'd be good at that." Shaking his head, he added, "I admire your ingenuity. You'll do just fine in life, Myla." With that declaration, he finished the last bite of his cake.

Myla turned back to her cooking. She had to stop watching this man eat. She wanted to cook him hearty meals and take care of him. He needed more than a housekeeper; he needed a spiritual partner. And after ten years of marriage to Sonny Howell, she wasn't sure she was ready for that yet.

Answering him finally, she said, "I have to do this, Nick. I have to provide for my children."

Nick put his empty plate and glass in the sink. "I believe you will. Patrick was right. You are a good cook."

"Thank you. Cooking's about all I have to offer." She faced him at last. "I need to tell you— the other job I came here to see about—it was a cook in a restaurant. I called today…and they've already hired someone."

Nick put a hand on her shoulder. "You found this job, Myla. Maybe…maybe you'll be better off here, for now." Not sure how to comfort her, he added, "And hey, if you keep this up, I'll be as fat as Santa by Christmas."

She laughed then. "You can work it off by starting that fire Patrick and Jesse want."

"Good idea. I rarely build a fire for just myself." He headed toward the swinging doors, then whirled. "By the way, how's Shredder doing?"

"He won't come out of Henny's apartment."

She waited, but when he just stood staring over at her, she asked, "Is there anything else, Nick?"

"Yes," he said, lowering his head a bit. "You're wrong, you know."

"About what?"

"Cooking isn't the only thing you have to offer, Myla."

He turned to go, leaving her to wonder what he'd meant by that statement. *Careful, Myla,* an inner voice warned. Nick was just being polite, trying to boost her ego. He didn't know anything about her, and right now, she didn't have the nerve to tell him the truth.

An hour later, Nick looked at the place set for one in the formal dining room. In spite of the Christmas centerpiece sitting in the middle of the long, shining Queen Anne table, the room still seemed empty and vast. In spite of the plate of steaming vegetables and hot-buttered noodles, the baked chicken and delicate dinner rolls, he couldn't seem to get excited about eating.

Too much cake, he reasoned, plopping down on an antique chair to try to enjoy Myla's marvelous efforts. "At last, peace and quiet."

With his first bite, he heard Myla's soft voice lifted in prayer. She was blessing their food in the other room. Sheepishly, Nick closed his eyes and listened. Glad when she'd finished, he whispered his own animated "Amen," then straightened his linen dinner napkin to get on with his meal.

Before he got a bite of succulent chicken between his teeth, he heard giggles from the kitchen, followed by voices all talking at once. They were a close trio, his little pack of strays. Myla seemed very protective of her children. Nick had to wonder what kind of man would leave her and her two children with nothing.

It's not your problem, Nick, he reminded himself. Sit up straight and eat your dinner.

With his first bite of the flaky roll, he remembered holding Myla the night before. Somehow, he'd managed to lose all decorum right there in his own kitchen. Carolyn would just love to have the details of that.

Of course, he didn't owe Carolyn or anyone else any explanations. He liked having no strings attached, and no obligations to anyone. Memories of his loving parents moved through the room like ghosts, haunting Nick with a poignancy he refused to acknowledge. He couldn't deal with the responsibilities of that kind of devoted love. He had other obligations—to Lydia and Rudolph Oil. Wishing Lydia didn't always work so late, he tried once again to eat his dinner.

By his third bite, Nick could stand it no longer. Used to his house being quiet, he hopped up on the pretense of telling them to keep it down so he could eat. Making a beeline for the swinging door, he opened it to find three sets of surprised eyes looking at him as if he were the abominable snowman.

"Are we bothering you?" Myla asked, jumping up to take the glass he had in his hand. "Can I get you anything?"

Nick threw up his hands. "Yeah, a chair. You all are having entirely too much fun in here. I decided I'd better eat in here with you, just so we could avoid anymore surprises like last night's."

"Sure!" Patrick patted the stool nearest him. "Come on in, Mr. Nick. We don't mind him eating with us, do we, Mom?"

"Of course not," Myla replied softly. "After all, this is his house. He can eat in any room he chooses."

Nick's smile spread across his face like cream over strawberries. "I'll go get my food."

In a few minutes, he was settled in, packing

away Myla's dinner like a man starved. Between bites, he regaled the children with tales of the adventures of Lydia and Nick as they were growing up.

"See this scar?" He showed Jesse a faint white dent right in the middle of his forehead. "Lydia gave me that with a roller skate. Had to have seven stitches. Mother made both of us go to bed early for a month."

"Why'd she hit you with a roller skate?" Jesse asked, her hoarseness making her voice soft-pitched.

"I chased her with a granddaddy long-legs," he explained, a grin encasing his face. "She hates spiders."

"I'm not scared of bugs," Jesse stated. "We lived in the country. I played with bugs all the time."

"Yeah, but we don't have that house no more, Jesse," Patrick reminded his sister. "It was repo—repur—"

"Repossessed," Myla finished, the flush on her cheeks indicating her discomfort. "Hush up now, and finish your dinner. We have to get up early tomorrow to get you both enrolled in school."

Nick steered the conversation away from the house they'd lost. "School? You two are too smart for that, aren't you?"

"Lydia's helping me get them straightened

out," Myla said over the children's giggles. "She's been such a help—she's even looking into low-cost housing in this district, in case I don't get into Magnolia House."

"Trust good ol' Lydia," Nick replied.

Wondering why he sounded so sarcastic, Myla said, "You don't share the same strong faith as your sister, do you?"

Shocked by her directness, Nick became defensive. "I've learned to rely on myself. I don't need to turn to a higher being to help me through life."

Myla leaned forward on her stool, her voice quiet. "Being self-reliant is good. After all, the Lord gave us brains. But sometimes, Nick, we can't do it all by ourselves. We need His help. And it's all right to ask for it."

She could see the anger sparking through his eyes.

"I don't need His help." Waving his arms, he spanned the room. "As you can see, I'm doing okay on my own."

She nodded. "Oh, yes, you're doing great material-wise. But what about spiritually? You don't like Christmas. Why is that, Nick?"

"That's none of your business," he said, getting up to stomp to the sink. "Your job is to run this house efficiently, not delve into my personal life."

She followed him. "Of course. You make perfect sense." She started stacking the dishes he absently handed her. "But then, you're in charge, right?"

"And what does that mean?" They stood shoulder to shoulder, heads up, eyes flashing.

"I know what's expected of me here, Nick. I work for you and I intend to do a thorough job. But I can't help but notice you don't have a strong sense of faith. That bothers me."

Wanting to turn the tables on her, he said, "Yeah, well, you need to be more concerned with your own problems. After all, you're the one without a home!"

Hurt, she said, "I'll find one. And I'll find a good job, too."

He groaned as she almost sliced his palm with a knife in her haste to load the dishwasher. "You'll barely make ends meet, Myla. It's going to be a struggle."

"I'll manage," she retorted. "I have a higher help than you'll ever know."

"Oh, that's right. Your faith. Well, faith won't get you through a cold winter night, now will it?"

"It did," she replied calmly. "I prayed for help and the Lord sent it." She gave him a meaningful look.

"Fine," he said, sighing in defeat. "So, why

can't you just do the job you were hired to do, instead of wasting your time trying to save me?"

"I just thought you could use a friend."

"I don't need a friend, and you need to concentrate on getting your own life back in order."

"I will, but in the meantime, if you need to talk…"

"I don't need anything, Myla." Trying to change the focus back to her, he added, "I'm willing to help you in any way I can, though. And I'm worried about you moving into that homeless shelter too soon. Having faith is one thing, but surviving is quite another."

"I would think you'd want me to move out," she replied. "You spout all this encouragement, then hand me a few checks to cover your own embarrassment. I'm trying to start over—on my own, and while I appreciate everything you and Lydia and your friends are doing, I have to do this for myself. If that means giving myself over to blind faith, if that means putting my trust in the Lord, then I can do it. I won't let anyone ever make me question my faith again." She stopped loading dishes to stare across the room at her two suddenly quiet children.

"What do you mean?" Nick asked, his hand on her arm. "What happened between you and your husband, Myla?"

"I…we'll talk later, maybe." Pulling away, she

called to the children. "Jesse, Patrick, time for bed."

Patrick immediately followed Myla to Henny's room, but Jesse held back. Running up to Nick, she tugged on his jeans. "Daddy wasn't a bad man, Mr. Nick. Momma told us to always remember that. My Daddy wasn't a bad man. He just had some problems, is all."

"Jesse!" Myla's voice echoed through the house.

The little girl ran away before Nick could question her further. What did all this mean? Up until now, he'd believed Myla to be a grieving widow, but there was obviously more to this.

"Who are you really protecting, Myla?" he whispered. "Yourself and your children? Or your dead husband?"

Chapter Four

The next week passed in a busy rush for Myla. After getting the children back in school, and finding a church nearby to attend while she was working for Nick, she fell into the daily routine of cleaning and cooking, and learning more about Nick's life. Each detail drew her closer to the man who'd reluctantly saved her from the streets, and each detail showed her that Nick needed to find his own faith again. He'd refused her invitation to attend church.

"I send them a hefty check each month," he informed her. "I catch up on paperwork on Sundays."

"You should rest, and spend the day in worship," she replied. And have some fun, she wanted to add.

He'd shot her one of his famous scowls, but

his words hadn't been as harsh as he'd have her believe. "You should mind your own business."

"Yes, sir." She certainly knew her place, and she needed the money. She'd have to be more cautious in her resolve to help him spiritually. And more cautious about her growing feelings for her employer.

But how could she resist being drawn to this intriguing man? She watched him leaving the house in a hurry each morning at the crack of dawn. He hardly bothered to stop and sip the coffee and orange juice she had waiting. She watched him come dragging in at night to wolf down the dinners she prepared before he went straight into his spacious office and clicked on the computer. Nick often worked long into the night. She knew, because she couldn't sleep very well in her new surroundings and she'd seen the light on in his office many times.

Myla had had an instinctive urge to go and check on Nick in the middle of the night, the way she used to do with her late husband. But that wasn't part of her official duties. And neither was being so attracted to him.

Her duties this morning involved cleaning the master bedroom. As she stood in the wide upper hallway, she prayed for guidance.

Dear Lord, give me the strength to get my

*work done, and not think about the man who's
helped me so much.*

But the minute she entered the big masculine
room decorated with tasteful plaids and subtle
stripes, Nick's presence shouted out at her. His
suit from yesterday was draped across the standing valet. Out of habit, she brushed it out and
hung it up, so he could wear it once more before
she took it to the cleaners.

His shoes were shelved in the long, well-
lit closet off the dressing room. He had several pairs, some black and brown leather, some
gleaming white athletics, all expensive and clas-
sic in design, just like their owner. His shirt, im-
peccably white, was tossed on a chair, waiting to
be laundered and pressed at the cleaners, along
with all his other tailored shirts.

So much about Nick's habits reminded her of
Sonny. Sonny had been a perfectionist, almost
fanatical in his demands. Nick wasn't quite that
bad, as far as she could tell. He demanded loy-
alty, hard work, and the best in everything—but
he demanded those things in himself first and
foremost.

Myla picked up the shirt, catching the scent
of his spicy, crisp aftershave. The shirt spoke of
the man. Solid, honest, clean. And lost. He was
a good man, but he was a lonely, sad man. His

quiet, aloof nature drew her to him, then his rare burst-through smiles and dry humor held her.

She couldn't fight her feelings, but she reminded herself she'd been on the bottom for so long, coming up for air was scary. She couldn't read anything into Nick's smiles and concerned gestures. He was just being kind. And he was used to having someone wait on him hand and foot. He was selfish and stubborn at times, and other times, he was caring and compassionate. Just his nature. She didn't think she was ready to deal with another domineering male just yet, though.

"Come on, Myla," she told herself as she hastily cleaned the large, elegant room. "You work for him. He gave you a job and a place to stay and food for your children. Nothing more. He owes you nothing."

Since she was alone in a twenty-room mansion, she could talk out loud. "And I owe him everything."

Silently, she thanked the Lord for giving her this reprieve and remembered that she'd promised to do things differently this time.

Moving into the bathroom, she cleaned the large garden tub with a new vigor, putting images of Nick Rudolph's handsome face out of her mind. Then she hurried out of the room, determined to stick to business.

And ran right smack into the arms of the very man she was trying to escape.

Myla's dust rag and cleaning supplies went in one direction and her armful of laundry went in the other as she plowed into Nick, sending him back against the sturdy oak railing on the second floor landing.

Catching her just as his back hit the banister, Nick gripped her shoulders to keep both of them from toppling down the stairs. "Goodness, is there a fire in there?"

She leaned against him in relief. "Nick, you scared me!"

"I'll say. Are you all right?"

Myla glanced up at him, embarrassed and acutely aware of his arms holding her. She had to learn not to be so clumsy! "I'm fine. What are you doing home so early?"

Nick hesitated, his smile as wry as ever. Then she noticed with a mother's keen eye, he looked flushed and his dark eyes were glazed over with a red-rimmed heat.

Concerned, she automatically put a palm to his forehead. "Why, you're burning up with fever!"

He pushed her away with a gentle shove. "Tell me something I don't know. Don't get too close. According to my friend and racquetball partner,

Dr. Loeffler, I've got the flu. That's the only way he'd ever beat me and he knows it."

Myla kicked her scattered cleaning supplies out of the way and steered him toward his room. "You went to work like this, and played racquetball! Honestly, don't you ever know when to quit?"

He drew his brows together, amused at her righteous indignation and her bossy nature. "I felt kind of tired this morning, but things got progressively worse as the day wore on. Dr. Loeffler checked me over after our game and told me to get home. Guess he couldn't believe he'd actually beaten me."

Myla clucked over him with all the vigor of a mother hen. "Will you stop making jokes and get into bed? I'll make you some chicken soup and get you some medicine for that fever. What did the doctor tell you to do?"

Nick gave her a lopsided grin. "He told me to let a beautiful woman serve me chicken soup and give me something for my fever."

Laughter bubbled in her throat, but she managed to keep her tone stern. "You're impossible. You'd better be all tucked in when I come back."

"Yes, ma'am, Nurse Myla."

She put both hands on her hips. "And don't expect me to baby you. I'm busy and you need to rest. I know you must really feel horrible. You never come home early."

He sent her a mock scowl. "No, I don't, but I still intend to get some work done. So, hand me my briefcase before you head down to concoct your flu survival kit."

Hissing her disapproval, she picked up the heavy leather satchel he'd left on a chair. Shoving it at his midsection, she said, "You do love your work, that's for sure."

Nick watched as she pranced out of the room, then he dropped like a lead weight onto the big bed. Holding his hands around the stuffed briefcase, he nodded to himself. He did love his work, but right now it was the last thing on his mind.

He fell back in a heap against the fluffy plaid pillows. Well, if a man's gotta be sick, he reflected with a grin, at least it helps to have a spunky redheaded nurse waiting on him hand and foot. This might turn out to be a good thing. He could actually enjoy being here, that is, if his body would just stop hurting all over.

A few minutes later, Myla was back with the promised soup and medicine, glad to see he was dressed in a blue sweat suit. He sat propped against pillows with paperwork scattered all around him, and a laptop computer centered in front of him on the bed.

"Are you going to eat and then rest?" she questioned as she set the bed tray down in front of him, then pulled the laptop away.

Giving her a mock angry glare, he brought the laptop back beside him. "Can you spoon-feed me?" he teased, enjoying the way her denim skirt whirled around her boots as she fussed with his discarded clothes.

"I don't think so," she retorted, a smile creasing her lips in spite of her reprimanding look. "You don't seem that weak to me."

"Gee, such a caring nurse."

"I'm sorry," she finally said, taking his droll humor seriously. "I'm just not used to you being home during the day. You've thrown me completely off schedule."

Nick knew his smile was awfully smug. He'd also brought a becoming blush to her apple cheeks. He liked knowing that his presence distracted her. That meant she was interested. Although, he reassured himself as he watched the winter sun dancing off her radiant auburn hair, he really didn't have time to indulge in a relationship. And he had no earthly idea where this one was going.

He put the laptop aside, then sampled the soup before sitting back to stare up at her. "I think you're just not used to me, period. But I'd say, all in all, this arrangement is working out okay.

Other than that one unfortunate incident with Shredder and that overgrown puppy of Carolyn's, you and the children haven't been any trouble, if that's what you're worried about."

"I'm not," she said, backing away, memories of being in his arms in the middle of the kitchen floor reminding her that she needed to concentrate on her job. "I'd better get back to work."

"Myla, wait." He gave her a questioning look. "Tell me how you do it?"

A look of confusion colored her green eyes. "Do what?"

"Keep that serene expression on your face. After everything you've been through, including putting up with my demands, you seem so at peace."

She looked up then, her not-so-serene gaze meeting his. "I found my strength again," she said simply. "I found my faith again, after I thought I'd lost it forever."

Uncomfortable with this turn in the conversation, he said, "How'd you manage a thing like that?"

She lifted her chin. "Prayer. You know, Nick, when you have nothing left, you always have prayer."

No, he didn't know that. It had been a very long time since he'd relied on prayer. "Why... how did you lose your strength?"

She backed farther away, like a frightened bird about to take flight. "I don't want to discuss that."

"I'd really like to know…and to understand."

When she didn't answer immediately, he said, "Look, I'll take my medicine, and I promise I'll eat my soup. Sit down in that chair over there and talk to me."

Myla hesitated only a minute. Wanting him to see that he, too, could find his strength in faith, she sat down and watched as he diligently took two pills with a glass of juice; then, his eyes on her, he dutifully ate his soup.

Satisfied that he'd finish the soup, she leaned back for a minute. "You see, at one time, I thought God had abandoned me."

Surprised, he stopped eating. Funny, he'd thought that very thing himself, right after burying his father. "Why would you think that? You seem so sure about all this religious stuff."

She lowered her head, her hands wringing together, her eyes misty with memories. "I wasn't so sure for a while. Because of something I did, or rather, something I didn't do—and I'd rather not talk about it. It took me a long time to see that God hadn't abandoned me. It was the other way around."

"You mean, you abandoned Him?"

She nodded. "I gave up on Him. I didn't think I was worthy of His love."

"Why would you think a thing like that?"

"I had it drummed into me enough," she said, then gasped. "Oh, never mind. I shouldn't have said that."

"Well, you did. What do you mean?"

When she didn't speak, Nick sat up to stare across at her. "Does this have something to do with your husband?"

Her silence told him everything he needed to know. And brought out all the protective instincts he'd tried so hard to ignore. "Myla, did your husband do something to hurt you?"

Myla didn't want to cry. She'd learned not to cry. But now, after she'd heard Nick voice the truth, her worst secrets floated up to the surface of her consciousness, causing the tears to roll down her cheeks like a torrent of rain coming from a black cloud. Holding her eyes tightly shut, she tried to block out the painful memories. She couldn't let him see her like this. Lifting out of the chair, she said, "I need to get back to work."

Nick moved his tray away with a clatter and stood up. "Myla, did you and he…was it a good marriage?"

She bit her bottom lip, then gave him a soul-weary look. "In the beginning, yes. But, it turned ugly after a few years."

Nick closed his eyes, then opened them to look at her with dread. "Did he...did he abuse you?"

She brought her hands up to her face and cried softly.

Nick pulled her hands away, his eyes searching her face. "Did he?"

"No, not physically," she said, her hands automatically gripping his. "Nick, please don't make me talk about this now." She didn't want the bond they had developed to be destroyed, not yet.

"I want...I need to know," he said, his voice husky, his words gentle. "I won't judge you, Myla."

But she was afraid he would, just as so many others had. "I'm...not ready to tell you everything."

The pain in her green eyes stopped Nick from pushing her any further. Instead, he said, "What can I do, to help you?"

She looked up at him, unable to ask for his help, unable to ask for his understanding.

But Nick knew instinctively that she needed both. So before she could bolt, he tugged her into his arms and rocked her gently, as if she were a child who needed reassuring. "No more questions," he prom-ised. "But if you want to cry, you go right ahead."

Myla did cry. Shutting her eyes tightly closed, she let him hold her for a while, thankful that he didn't press her any further about her marriage. Just to be held, unconditionally, that was comfort enough for now.

"All right," he said after a while, letting go to pat her shoulder. "Feel better now?" At her silent nod, he added, "You can't keep this inside. Lydia knows people, therapists and counselors, who can help you. And…I want to help, too."

She lifted her head, then wiped her eyes with the back of her hand, resolve settling back over her like a protective winter cloak. With a shaky smile, she said, "You're a fine one to be giving me advice. I am a lot better now, though, really."

He looked doubtful. "How can you say that?"

"I told you, I found my faith again—alone, on a dark cold night. I was huddled in the car with the children, with nothing left…nothing. In the moonlight, I saw my worn Bible lying on the dashboard. I hadn't read it in months. I did that night, though, with a flashlight. While my children slept in the cold, I found my faith again in that single beam of light, and I cried long and hard, and I prayed, really prayed, for the first time in a very long time."

Nick swallowed back the lump forming in his throat. "What did you find there in that light, that helped you?"

She sniffed, then lifted her head. "He said He would not leave me comfortless, but I had forgotten that promise. In First Corinthians, chapter thirteen, verse thirteen, the Bible says, 'And now abideth faith, hope, love, these three: but the greatest of these is love'."

Nick stood there, his heart trembling. Love. The one thing he'd been so afraid of since his father's breakdown and death. "How did that verse sustain you?"

She smiled then. "I knew that no matter what, I had my children with me and I loved them above all else, except the Lord. They were my gift, and no matter what kind of life I'd had with their father, they were my responsibility. Love, Nick. Love is the greatest gift of all. It gives us our strength. It gives us a reason to go on living, even when we'd rather curl up and sleep. I realized that God gave us unconditional love when He sent His son to save us from our sins. I realized that God hadn't abandoned me. He was reaching out to me on that dark night."

Nick sighed, his own fears cresting in the midst of her eloquent story. "But…unconditional love is so hard to give and so very hard to expect. To love so completely, you have to give up so much control. How can you trust something that abstract, something that can make you seem so weak?"

"That's the whole point," she said, her expression changing from sorrowful to hopeful. "Love doesn't make us weak, Nick. Love gives us the strength to go on. That night, alone and afraid, I remembered God's unconditional love for me. I'd lost that, as well as my trust. I'd been emotionally stripped of that love and that trust, by a man who didn't know how to give either."

"Your husband."

She nodded, then stepped back. "I'm all right now. I won't be afraid of the dark, ever again. I made a promise to take care of my children. They don't deserve to have to live like this—they didn't do anything wrong."

"Neither did you. You seem so brave. Is that for your children's sake?"

"I have to be strong, for them."

Nick felt his heart melting in half. He'd never seen such a fierce defense of love, or heard such a strong testimony. She had come to him with nothing, yet she had more to give than any woman he'd ever known. "Is there anything I can do?"

Unable to look at him, Myla couldn't speak about her pain. Leaning close, she whispered, "Just hold me again."

He did, for a long while, his arms wrapping her in what little protection he could offer. Finally, he brought a hand up to her chin so he could wipe her tears away. Gazing down at her, Nick wanted badly to kiss her.

But Myla stood back, her voice clear once again. "You'd better rest. And I'd better get away from you. I don't have time to get the flu."

He laughed at that. "Always the practical one." Leaning back down on the bed, he added, "I am feeling a little wobbly. Are you sure you're all right?"

"I'm fine now," she said as she lifted his tray away, her eyes downcast. "Do you need anything else?"

He looked up at her, thinking how right it seemed to have her here with him, thinking he needed her strength. "No, thanks. You've spoiled me quite enough, I believe."

His words soothed Myla like a balm. "Nick?" she called from the door.

"Hmmm?"

"Thank you, for understanding."

He wanted to tell her he didn't understand, really. But the weight of sleep blocked out his reply. He didn't understand how one minute he could be so sure, so secure in his firm, smug convictions, then the next, begin to doubt everything he stood for.

He wasn't as fearful as he should be. He wasn't so much afraid of reaching out for love now. Myla had done that for him. She'd opened up her heart and told him a story of faith that left him humbled and ashamed. For so long now, he'd been afraid of the power of love. He'd believed loving someone could make a person weak, just as his grieving, dying father had become. But he'd been so very wrong. Nick needed to hold Myla again, just to be held himself.

Instead, he reached for his pillow and buried his dreams and his doubts in a deep, troubled sleep.

Nick woke hours later to find his room dark, except for the flickering light from the fire someone had lit in the sitting area fireplace. The room was cozy, but a flash of thunder and lightning told of the wintry chill settling over the city. He shuddered to think Myla and her children could have been out there, alone, in that cold night. And he wondered how many people were cold and shivering and afraid this night.

Groaning, Nick rolled over, acutely aware of his own discomfort. This was a mean flu bug, that was for sure.

His throat felt like he'd swallowed a jalapeño pepper and his head throbbed with each beat of his pulse. Craving a long, hot shower, he rose to calculate the distance to the bathroom. A bold knock hit the bedroom door before he could attempt the trip, causing a ricocheting rumble in his head.

"Come in," he called in a raspy voice.

Lydia popped her head in the door. "Well, big brother, sleeping the day away won't get your Christmas shopping done."

He moaned, rolling over to face the fire. "Go away."

"Glad you're feeling better," she replied as she tossed him a bag of prescription medicines. "Dr. Loeffler sent you these—antibiotics and a decongestant. He said to take all of it."

"He's just trying to poison me so I won't beat him at racquetball again." Giving her a false smile, he added, "I don't like being sick."

Lydia handed him two drawings. "Maybe these will cheer you up."

Nick grinned. Jesse had reproduced the kitchen disaster, complete with Shredder sitting on the ceiling fan and Pooky lapping away amidst a pile of food. Patrick had drawn a Christmas tree loaded with colorful gifts.

"Your two biggest fans send their regards. Aren't those two adorable?"

Nick laid the pictures on the nightstand. "Yeah, and very well-behaved, as far as children go. Lydia, has Myla told you anything about their past?"

"A little. Why?"

"We had a long talk today. She's had a rough

time, but she won't tell me exactly what happened in her marriage."

Lydia sat down to stare at her brother. "Well, don't press her. I introduced her to Reverend Hillard. I'm sure he can give her some spiritual guidance."

"Maybe," Nick said, remembering the story Myla had told him. "But I think her faith's intact. It's her self-esteem I'm worried about."

Lydia sat up, her eyes squinting toward him. "You're worse off than I thought. Did I hear you say something good about someone's faith? And that you're actually aware of another person's mental stability?"

He nodded, then shot her a wry smile. "Yes, you did. I want to help her, Lydia. She's a good woman."

"Well, praise the Lord." Lydia hopped up to give her brother a breath-stopping hug. "Oh, Nicky, I knew you'd come around. You really want to help, really, really?"

"Yes, really, really," he said, laughing. "I'd be a real Scrooge if I didn't see how much Myla and her children have been through. But don't make more out of this than it is. I think this flu's gone to my head."

"Or maybe Myla's gone to your heart," Lydia said softly. "After all, it is Christmas. A time for miracles."

He patted her on the back. "I'd forgotten what a joyous time it can be. And I'm sorry, really sorry, for being so hard to live with since Father's death."

She kissed him on the temple. "No need to apologize. Welcome back, Nick."

When Nick came out of the bathroom, his food was sitting on a tray in front of the leather armchair by the fireplace. Glancing around, he was disappointed that Myla wasn't there to make sure he ate everything on his plate. He still had a lot of questions to ask her.

Lydia was right. He did have a soft spot in his heart for Myla and her two children. And the spot was opening to include other possibilities such as attending church and opening the Bible he'd tossed aside years ago.

He should be scared, yet when he searched for the old fear, he only found a new, growing strength. Now, he was beginning to dread the time when Myla would have to leave.

Two weeks until Christmas. Usually, this old house was hushed and quiet around this time of year, haunted by the memory of his parents. Not this year. This year, things were going to be different.

A soft knock at the door caused him to put down the spoonful of beef stew he'd been about to eat. Two reddish blond heads bobbed just above the ornate door handle. Patrick and Jesse eyed him curiously.

"You two going to stand out in the hall all night, or are you going to get in here before your mother catches you?"

"We ain't supposed to be here," Patrick said in a small whisper. "But we wanted to say hi."

"It's *aren't*—we *aren't* supposed to be here," Jesse corrected as she pushed Patrick into the room.

Patrick made a face at his sister's redundancy. "I know that. That's what I just said."

"Where's your mother?" Nick asked, smiling at them.

Jesse tossed her ponytail. "Talking to Miss Lydia. Mama's gonna go to school at night and she's looking for another job, for when Miss Henny comes home. We'll just have to live in the shelter for a while, that's all."

Nick didn't want to think about that, so he changed the subject to more pleasant things. "Well, Santa'll be coming soon," he said, hoping to find two worthy allies in the children. "What do you want him to bring you?"

Both children rushed to his side, talking at once. Nick heard it all, registered each request and vowed to travel to the North Pole if he had to, just to get them all the loot they wanted.

"And what about your mom?"

"Oh, that's kinda hard," Jesse said, giggling. "Mama wants stuff you can't find in the mall."

"Yeah, like what?"

Jesse settled down on the floor, wiping her nose with her hand. "She wants a house, of course. She talks about having a home of her own again. And she wants a job. She doesn't like not having any money. Oh, and once, she told us she'd like a long soak in a tub of hot water, then get dressed up in a pretty green dress for a special Christmas dinner. She loves to cook, you know."

Nick once again marveled at the simple things he'd taken for granted. Clearing his suddenly clogged throat, he said, "Are you sure that's all she wants?"

Thinking for a minute, her nose scrunched, Jesse held her hands wide. "Oh, and roses. She loves yellow roses."

Patrick nodded. "Yeah, and one day, Daddy got real mad and mowed all of hers down."

Nick went still inside. Trying to keep his tone light and casual, he asked, "Why would he do a thing like that?"

"'Cause she didn't have dinner ready on time," Jesse said in a matter-of-fact voice. "She cried when he wasn't looking."

Dinner. No wonder she'd tried so hard to make

his dinner party a success. No wonder she'd been so shaken when it had gone bad. She was used to fixing things up, hiding her fear behind a false bravado.

Patrick pulled on Nick's sleeve, bringing him out of his numbed state. "I don't want much, Mr. Nick. I just wish we didn't have to leave here, ever."

Nick was beginning to wish that very same thing.

Before Nick could reply, however, the door swung open and Myla stomped into the room, a mother's wrath apparent in her expression. "What in the world! You two are supposed to be in bed! How'd you get up here?"

"We snuck by you," Patrick blurted out in spite of his sister's glaring look.

"That's obvious enough." Myla pointed a finger toward the door. "Get back downstairs with Miss Lydia. Do you both want to catch the flu?"

"I didn't breathe on them," Nick said, glad to find a light moment in the children's misdeeds. "And I'm glad they came by for a visit. I was getting downright lonely."

"Want us to stay awhile?" Patrick offered hopefully.

"No, he doesn't," his mother interjected. "Go on down. I'll come and read to you and help you with your prayers in a little while."

Nick managed a chuckle as he watched the children scoot out of the room. "Well, you certainly got rid of those two varmints."

She looked at his half-eaten food. "Why didn't you eat your supper?"

"I wasn't very hungry."

"Are you feeling better?"

"A little. I heard you and Lydia were plotting down there."

"Planning," she corrected. "There's a difference."

"I've never looked at it that way."

She started to take the tray, but his hand shot out to stop her. "Myla, could we talk some more?"

"No," she said, not daring to look at him. "I'd rather not."

"I won't press you about your life before," he said. "I just have some questions, about…this unconditional love about which you speak so highly."

She glanced up then, her eyes wide. "You want to discuss…religion?"

"Yes," he said, smiling slightly. "I think I'd like that."

And so they talked. She told him the stories of the Bible that he'd forgotten. As she talked, memories washed over him; memories of his mother, telling him these very same stories, her faith as strong and as shining as Myla's. How could he have forgotten the beauty in that? How could he have let it slip so far away?

After Myla said a gentle prayer for him to feel better, both physically and spiritually, he sat in the darkness alone, watching the fire. And realized he was tired of being alone in the dark.

Then it hit him—Myla had said something earlier about being afraid of the darkness. They were so alike, he and his Myla. They'd both been out in the cold for too long. Together, maybe they could find the warmth of that unconditional love she'd told him about. Together, with the help of a higher being watching over them.

Outside, the rain fell in cold, indiscriminate sheets and Nick shuddered, thinking again that she might have been out there tonight, all alone and frightened.

But she wasn't out there. For some strange reason, God had sent her to him instead. He wouldn't take that obligation lightly.

"Not again, Myla," he whispered to the fire. "Not ever again, if I can help it."

Then he did something he hadn't done in a very long time. He folded his hands and he prayed.

Chapter Five

It was well past midnight. Myla tiptoed into the kitchen, careful not to wake the children sleeping in the bedroom just down the narrow back hallway. With Nick being home sick the last couple of days, her mind was in turmoil. Sleep was impossible.

She didn't want to admit that she'd enjoyed playing nurse to him. The first morning, they'd talked and laughed together, sitting on the sunporch off the second-story hallway. Nick had insisted she sit with him while he had breakfast. It had been a comfortable, cozy distraction, complete with frolicking squirrels putting on a show in the great oaks lining the sloping backyard. Then, later in the day when he'd woken up feeling better, he'd come downstairs to eat a sandwich in the kitchen, reading the paper in silence while she went about her work. So domestic, so homey. So *wrong,* Myla reminded herself.

Setting the bags she carried on the counter, she pulled out the small treasures her first paycheck from Nick had allowed her to buy for her children. This would take her mind off of dreaming about a man she shouldn't be thinking about.

A sweater set for Jesse—pink-and-blue striped with little white bows on the Peter Pan collar. An inexpensive fashion doll with two sets of clothes. Some new jeans and an action toy for Patrick, along with a set of army men with tanks and jeeps. It wasn't much, but they'd have something under the tree. This year especially, it was important to her that her children understand the real Christmas celebration, so she didn't want to make a big deal out of gift giving. Yet she couldn't help but breathe a sigh of relief tonight.

She'd had horrible visions of them spending Christmas out in the cold, or in a shelter. Now, thanks to Nick's kindness, they were going to be celebrating Christmas in this beautiful, rambling house. Thinking of how lucky they were to be safe and warm, she stood there letting the tears fall freely.

And that's how Nick found her.

Her back was turned toward him and she was wearing a worn, thick flannel robe, pink with blue faded flowers and small red heart-shaped designs which, in the moon's soft spotlight, reminded him of aged paper valentines. He felt as if he could watch her forever, but when he heard her soft intake of breath and saw her wipe at a tear, he went to her, touching her lightly on the arm.

"Are you all right?"

Myla jumped at his touch, surprise widening her eyes. "Nick! What are you doing up?"

"Shredder woke me. That sneaky cat's taken a liking to me, I believe. He's also taken a liking to the foot of my bed, where I left him fast asleep."

She laughed then, but the laughter turned back to tears. "I'm sorry. I've been so emotional lately. Christmas always does that to me, but this year… well, I have a lot to be thankful for."

Nick once again felt the sharp contrast in her world and his own. "I can't imagine what it must have been like for you, out there. You're very courageous."

She sniffed back her tears. "Hardly. When it comes to survival, you just do what you've got to do."

"You're starting over," he said, careful of how he worded his next request. "Don't you think it's time you really left the past behind? Tell me everything about your marriage, Myla."

She looked up, deciding there in the darkness she could trust him with the truth. "Yes, I think it's time to move on, and I guess talking about it would help." Then she gave him one last chance.

"Are you sure you want me to burden you with the sordid details, though?"

"Burden away," he replied, his voice quiet and encouraging. "I won't be able to sleep if you don't tell me what's made you so sad."

She took a deep breath, then brought a hand up to play with one of the buttons on the front of her robe. "My husband deceived all of us. Sonny was a big fake, in complete control. And he had me trained as his robot. He even had the children trained, too. Only I didn't see it until it was too late."

"Tell me why."

She leaned back against the counter, her eyes shining. "I wish I knew why. Why I let him do the things he did, why I let him make me feel so small and helpless. Looking back, I think it was my need to please—my family, his family, our friends, him. I wanted to be a good wife, a good mother. That was my only ambition in life, because that's all Sonny wanted me to be. He'd convinced me that I wasn't very good at anything, but I thought at least I could be good at that. As it turned out, I didn't do such a hot job."

Nick took one of her hands. "Hey, who's doubting now? I can't believe you'd let anyone make you doubt yourself like that. You seem so capable, so strong."

"I wasn't always so surefooted," she said in a

whisper. "I did have doubts, and I'm so ashamed of what I let happen."

He shook his head. "It can't be that bad."

Pulling away, she headed to the refrigerator to pour two glasses of juice. Then she found the cookie jar and placed two fresh oatmeal cookies on a napkin for Nick. "It's so bad, I'm still ashamed to talk about it. Nick, Sonny embezzled funds from the bank he managed, and when the authorities found out…he committed suicide in his fancy car."

Nick could only stand there staring at her. The background check had only listed her as a bankrupt widow, just as she'd told him. "Myla, I had no idea."

"No, how could you? No one did. We went to church every Sunday, we had a nice ranch house in the country. We had everything. But it was all a sham. Sonny only played at being a Christian. He used church for networking and finding new clients. And when that didn't bring in enough money, he turned to crime.

"He had this obsessive need to always have more. More money, more power, all of the latest things—cellular phones, computers, any kind of gadget that would make him look successful. He never spent much time with the children—he had very little patience with them—but then he'd buy them all sorts of expensive toys to win their affection after he'd treated them badly. And I...I was so blind, so convinced that I had to work harder, try harder to be the perfect little wife, I didn't see that he was suffering, until it was too late. I never wanted more money or things. I wanted more of him, emotionally. But he couldn't give me that. And I didn't do anything to save him."

"But it's not your fault—"

"Yes," she said, bobbing her head. "Yes, it is. And I've been running ever since. From my family, because they blame me. From my so-called friends, because they can't be seen with me anymore. From myself, because I can't stand to look in the mirror each day. I had to protect my children, and that's the only thing that kept me going, until that night when I realized I wasn't alone." Looking up at him, she said, "Then, not too long after that night, I found you."

He turned to stand beside her as they both stared out into the bleak winter night. "So you've been struggling with this, all this time?"

She took a sip of juice, then set the glass down. "I kept thinking I should have done something to help Sonny."

"Help him? What could you have done?"

She turned, both hands braced on the counter. "I should have followed my instincts when I suspected something was wrong. But Sonny was hard to deal with even on a good day. He'd threaten me by telling me that I wasn't a good wife, and that it was my fault he felt so much pressure. Then he'd tell me he'd leave and take the children. I…I began to doubt my own Christianity. I mean, here I'd lived with this man for years and I'd believed he truly felt the same way I did, but he didn't. He put up this big front, but it was all an act. And I was too afraid to do anything about it, so I did what I had to, to protect my children."

"Why did you marry him?"

"I loved him, and I wanted a family. Sonny promised me we'd have a good life. He came from a wealthy family—his parents always over-indulged him—and I'd never had very much. It seemed like a dream. And turned into a nightmare. After he…after he died, I found out there was no money, no insurance, and most of the expensive things he'd bought got repossessed, right along with my house."

She faced him squarely now, her pride gone right along with all the fancy possessions and high hopes she'd once had. "I will always remember the day they came and locked up my house. The bank officer had been a friend of ours. He kept telling me how sorry he was, but he didn't really offer to make things any better. He was just doing his job.

"You don't forget that feeling, you don't forget the scorn and pity you see on people's faces. Ever. That's why, this time I intend to do things my way, with the help of the Lord. I won't ever let anyone make me doubt myself or my faith again."

Nick leaned close, his gaze sweeping her face. Unable to see his expression completely in the muted light, Myla waited, wondering if he, too, would turn away in disgust. But he didn't. Instead, he placed his hands on her face, his touch as soft as the moonlight, and then he kissed her.

The touch of his lips on hers was gentle, yet powerful. No one had reached out to her like this in a very long time. A soft, secure warmth spread through her, blocking out the cold night and the bad memories. As much as she needed this, Myla was still afraid to give in to the myriad feelings coursing through her system. She couldn't let herself become too dependent on this man's kindness.

Nick felt her tense up, heard the defeat in her soft sigh. Cupping his hands on her shoulders, he stared down at her. "You don't have to doubt me, Myla. I know I was completely indifferent when we met, but I've changed a lot since then. I want to help you through this."

She touched his face with her hand, hope warring with despair in her mind. "I know you do.

And you can, with your money, with your connections, but don't you see—that's the kind of help Sonny provided. He took care of me materially, but he was never there with me spiritually. I won't be a burden to anyone again. And I won't commit to anyone who can't go the distance with me. Right now, I'm still too battered to take things any further, Nick."

Nick stood there holding her, wondering if he, too, was afraid to take things any further. He'd certainly done a complete turnaround. But from the moment he'd looked into those luminous green eyes, he'd been hopelessly lost. Or maybe hopefully found.

Still struggling, still amazed, he said, "What about feelings? What about need?"

She gave him an imploring look. "Do you need me, Nick?"

"I think so," he said honestly. "But I'm moving into dangerous territory here. I've got to learn *how* to need someone."

Myla took their juice glasses to the sink, then turned to face him across the kitchen. "Maybe we both should step back and consider the consequences of our feelings. You've got everything a human could possibly need, but you've lost your faith. I've lost everything—all the comforts of home—but I've found my faith again. I won't have it stripped away, and I won't let you step in and take control the way Sonny always did."

"You think I'd do that to you?"

"No, you're not like him, but you're still fighting against your own feelings, and that could cause the same sort of resentment Sonny felt toward me. He teased me about my church work and my beliefs, then pretended he felt the same way when others were around. That hurt more than anything. I won't get into a battle of that kind with you. I won't make you choose. That has to be your own decision. And, needing me has to come from your heart, not from some sense of obligation or sympathy."

He moved across the kitchen to take her back into his arms. "I'm not so sure what I'm feeling right now, but I do know that it's not just an obligation to ease my hardened soul. I want to take care of you, but I understand how important it is for you to pull yourself out of this, both emotionally and financially. I should know—I've been doing that same thing since my father died."

"We've both been lost," Myla said, her gaze holding his.

Nick tugged her close then lifted a hand to touch her face again. "Right now, I don't feel so lost anymore." After a tender kiss, he told her, "But I do think I'm losing the battle, with you and with your mighty God."

"We have to be sure," she reminded him. "No matter how we feel about each other, there has to be a commitment to a third being in this relationship. That's the only way it can work."

Nick didn't reply. He knew she was right. She wouldn't live a lie again. This time, she wanted a commitment that meant turning control over to God, instead of letting another human being control her. It was a tall order, and one he'd have to give careful consideration and prayer.

"We'll make it work," he assured her. "We'll take it slow. I'm not a very patient man, but…I think I can learn to be."

Myla's heart soared as she gave him a chaste kiss on the cheek. "Thank you, for listening. And for not judging."

As he watched her walk down the hall, her long red hair trailing around her neck, Nick realized she might be the one without a place to live, but he was the one without a home.

"Mama, Mama, can we get up now?"

Myla rolled over, opening her eyes slowly to find her children sitting up in bed, watching her as if she knew all the secrets to life. Moaning, she sat up to wipe hair out of her eyes. "What time is it?"

"Six o'clock," Jesse said, reaching out to hug

Myla tightly. "Can we please see what Santa brought?"

Christmas morning. Myla hugged Jesse against her. "Sure, honey. Just let me get the sleep out of my eyes."

As the children jumped up and down in glee, Myla thought about the Christmas Eve service they'd all attended last night, including Nick.

"It's his first time in ten years," Lydia had explained, tears in her eyes. "Oh, Myla, this is the happiest Christmas we've had in a long time."

It had been happy for Myla, too. Reverend Hillard was a wonderful, compassionate preacher and a good listener. He'd helped her deal with her past through prayer and positive discussions. Then, to relive the Christmas miracle, to see the shining faces of faith in the muted light of hundreds of candles, had only renewed her own faith and strength. She'd come so far with God's help, and now, Nick, too, seemed to be finding a new strength. Could it be possible that God had brought them together to help each other heal?

But she had to remind herself, she was still fearful of depending too much on anyone else to help her back on her feet. Especially Nick, since he still seemed so unsure himself.

After church, he'd dropped them off back at the house, then after making some excuse about putting in an obligatory appearance, had headed out to a party at Carolyn's. Myla had never felt so lonely, sitting there watching her children sleep. Was Nick still fighting his feelings? Did seeing Carolyn only reinforce his need to stay in control?

But, Myla groggily reminded herself this morning, she had no hold over Nick, and soon, she'd be moving out anyway. God had a purpose for her, but maybe that purpose wasn't for Nick and her to be together. She'd have to leave that in God's hands.

"Mom, hurry," Patrick whined from his perch at the foot of the bed, his cartoon-character pajamas as bright as the glow in his eyes.

"Hold on, sweetie." As she washed her face and tugged on her clothes, Myla said a prayer for guidance.

Help me to do Your will, and guide me in my feelings for Nick. If You want us to be together, give Nick the strength to learn to love. Show me the way, Lord, and give me the courage to walk away from him if I have to make that choice.

"Get up, Nick!"

Lydia yanked the covers back, sending a cold rush of air into Nick's warm, sleep-covered world.

"Why do you always have to stalk into my bedroom and bother me?" he asked, groping for the blankets as he took in her bright red flannel pajamas. "And do you have to look so jolly?"

Lydia held the blankets away. "I heard the pitter-patter of little feet downstairs. You wanted to be awake and alert for the big event, remember?"

"I remember."

"Well, get moving. I want to see them when they find all that loot you bought for them."

He'd only meant to buy the children a few toys, not a truckload. "Did I go overboard?"

"That's an understatement, big brother. But I seriously doubt the local toy store is complaining. You made them go over the top in sales, I'm sure."

Nick sat up, then gave his sister a sleepy stare. "Lydia, I've been meaning to ask you—has Myla talked to you any more about her marriage?"

Lydia's usually perky face became guarded. "What do you mean?"

"She has, hasn't she? Lydia, I want to know what's going on with her. I mean, she told me what happened, with her husband's suicide and all. But, I need to know—is she healing now? Or does she still feel guilty?"

He didn't want to scare Myla away, but he had to know if she was really feeling better about things, because his own patience was wearing thin. He wanted to nurture her and protect her, yet he held back, waiting, hoping.

"That's very personal, Nick. And you know I can't discuss that with you." Sitting down on the bed, she said, "Please, don't press her on this. Women who've been through that kind of pain…it takes a while for them to trust again." Maneuvering him back to the task at hand, she added, "But, at least she's been receiving counseling from Reverend Hillard. That's so important for her state of mind." Then, changing the subject with expert ease, she added, "And at least she can't fault *you* in the gift-giving department. Now, hurry up!"

Nick went into the bathroom to wash his face and toss on his clothes. Minutes later, he came back, dressed in khakis and a sweater, and worried that he'd made a big mistake. "I just wanted them to have a good Christmas. Think Myla will mind?"

Lydia extended a hand to him as he emerged. "Only one way to find out." Hugging him close, she said, "Merry Christmas, Nick."

The sound of squealing children greeted Nick and Lydia as they entered the double doors to the den. The room was in total chaos. Wrapping paper and toys decorated its usually sedate interior.

Lydia patted her brother's neck, then pushed

him into the room. "My, my, sure looks like Santa came here."

Patrick looked up from the gigantic toy train that whistled as it sped around the Christmas tree. "Look, Mr. Nick. Santa brought me a train and some boots and a farm set. How'd he know we used to live on a farm, anyway?"

"Santa's very smart," Nick said, his eyes meeting Myla's. She stood in the corner by the window, her expression tight-lipped, her face pale.

"He gave me a mermaid doll that sings," Jesse shouted, running up to Nick and Lydia to proudly display the beautiful doll. "And a dollhouse."

Lydia fell to the floor, exploring the treasures as if she were only eight years old herself. Holding up the less expensive doll Myla had bought for Jesse, she asked, "Who's this?"

"I don't know her name," Jesse replied, her attention on the other toys surrounding her.

"She's very pretty," Lydia coaxed, her gaze flying up to meet Nick's.

He looked from her to Myla, his heart sinking. Uh-huh, he'd blown this one, big-time. What had he been thinking?

Myla pivoted to head for the kitchen. "I'll go make some coffee."

Nick followed, ready to apologize for his excessiveness. He winced as she yanked the refrigerator door open and pulled out a huge can of coffee. Taking a deep breath, he stopped her before she could bring the scoop to the filter cup. "I'm sorry, Myla."

Myla set the scoop full of coffee down with a shaking hand. "How could you, Nick? After I told you how I felt…after I told you how Sonny used to try and buy our affection."

"I…I got carried away," he tried to explain. "Christmas around here is usually so gloomy, and I wanted to do something special for the children."

Some of the anger left Myla. How could she be mad when he'd been so generous? Although she knew his motives were completely different from Sonny's, it still worried her that he had some of the same traits. "I know you meant well, Nick, but I can't have them thinking this is the way it's going to be from now on. A lot of expensive toys can't prepare them for the tough time we've got ahead of us. I want them to be children, to enjoy the wonder of Christmas morning, but I also want them to understand that Christmas is about more than getting toys."

"Of course," he agreed, helping her to finish making the coffee. "And I truly wasn't thinking. I never meant to overshadow what you'd already bought for them."

Myla turned on the oven and shoved in the coffee cake she'd made the day before. "I'm very grateful to you," she admitted, "but you have to understand how important this is to me."

"I do understand," he said, following her to the cabinet. "But it's important that you understand me, too. I'm trying to change, Myla. I've...I've been bitter and self-centered, and so preoccupied with work since my father's death, and you know how I am. I'm used to taking charge and telling everyone what to do."

At her knowing I-couldn't-agree-with-you-more glance, he hurried on. "This was a big step for me, to celebrate Christmas in any way at all. And to be able to give to someone, freely and with sincerity...well, it's been a long time since I've felt like this. Maybe I never knew what Christmas was all about myself, until now."

Myla had to swallow the lump in her throat. His admission reinforced what she already knew about him. Behind that indifferent exterior lay a heart of gold. A hurting heart. He had so much to give, much more than a pile of money. And he was trying hard to show her that, even if he had gone about it too excessively.

She stopped her busywork and turned to stare up at him, her eyes wide. "Oh, Nick, it was wonderful, watching their eyes light up when they ran into that room. What you did...it was so sweet, and I shouldn't be mad. But what am I supposed to do with all those wonderful gifts when we move into Magnolia House?"

"You've got a while," he said, not wanting to think about that. "And you can let them keep their things here and come back here anytime to play with the stuff until you get settled in your own place."

She placed her hand on his. "Christmas is here, Nick. In a few days, Henny will be back from Arkansas. We're on the list to move into the shelter. Lydia says we can move in soon, and after a few months, I should be able to find a low-income house with Lydia's help. I've still got a lot of hard work ahead of me."

He lowered his head, then held her hand tight against his. He couldn't tell her that he had no intention of letting her move into a homeless shelter. "I know—we agreed from the beginning this situation couldn't last. I guess I'd just conveniently forgotten about it."

No, that wasn't exactly true. He'd thought of nothing else, but he had to tread lightly here.

"Yes, we agreed this was only a temporary arrangement," she reminded him. "Don't make it any harder for me, please?"

He saw the pain in her eyes, saw the plea to let her go peacefully, without a big fuss. How could he do that now, when she'd opened up his heart and staked a claim on him? But her firm resolve told him he didn't have any control here, none at all. "If you need any advice—"

She pulled her hand away, trying to ignore the little sensations coursing through her body. "Sonny always advised me. It's time I did things on my own."

That angered him. His voice deepening with each word, he said, "I'm not Sonny."

Lydia peeked in the swinging doors before Myla could reply. "Hey, everything all right in here?"

"Fine," Nick said, waving her away. "We'll be back in soon with some coffee cake."

That reminded Myla of the hot oven. With a wail, she hurried to check the cake. Smoke poured from the stove as she pulled the door open. "Oh, I forgot about it. It's ruined!"

Lydia stepped inside the kitchen, her eyes wide with disbelief. "Have you ever noticed when you two get together in the kitchen, something always goes wrong?"

Myla pulled the charred cake out of the oven, then rolled her eyes. "Too many cooks spoil the broth."

Patrick and Jesse came running. Patrick held up a bright green laser gun and aimed straight for the blackened cake, firing a noisy round of pretend lasers. "Got it," he said with a grin. "Gee, Mom, you used to know how to cook."

Myla looked at Nick, a smile twitching at the corner of her mouth in spite of her earlier concerns. He laughed, too, relaxing as the tension between them eased.

"Anyone for pizza?" Lydia asked, her eyes lifting skyward.

"Dinner was wonderful."

Nick's eyes met Myla's across the expanse of the Queen Anne dining table. He liked this. He liked having Lydia and the children here to share a big Christmas dinner. He didn't know when exactly he'd started liking it, but his mood was more in line with the holiday spirit because of Myla and her two children. Now if he could just convince her to stay here, with him.

"Thank you," Myla said in a hushed tone. Her mind kept going back to what Nick had said in the kitchen. He was changing. She could tell that. He'd even said grace before he carved the turkey for dinner. Still, she was reluctant to trust him completely. Yet when she sat here, looking at him, exchanging warm smiles at some cute comment from one of the children or just noticing how handsome he looked in his sweater and casual slacks, she knew it wouldn't take much for her to fall for him. Oh, this was so hard!

Lydia cleared her throat loudly, bringing

Myla's head up. "And the dressing...I love oyster dressing, don't you, Nick?"

"Yes, love it."

"Can I have a piece of pecan pie?" Patrick asked.

"You've barely touched your meal," Myla said, her eyes still on the man at the head of the table. "Considering we had a light breakfast, I'd say you'd better eat as much as you can."

"I did eat," Patrick whined. "I'm ready for pie."

"In a few minutes, Patrick."

Jesse tried. "I'm ready for pie, too, Mama."

Myla's gaze shifted from one child to the other. She couldn't help but smile. Jesse was almost completely well from her cold, and her children were well fed and warm. In many ways, this Christmas had been one of their best together. "Oh, all right. I guess you can have dessert now." Looking down the table, she saw Nick's grinning expression. "I suppose you want some pie, too?"

"Yes, Mom," he said, bursting out in laughter, then quickly clearing his throat to look serious. "If that's all right with you?"

Myla rose to get the requested goodies. "Of course. I didn't bake it for it to just sit there looking pretty."

After the children hopped up to follow their mother, Lydia gave her brother a curious look. "What's going on?"

"Nothing. Everything's great." He changed the subject. "Remember when you mentioned taking the children to see the Christmas lights at the American Rose Center?" At her confused nod, he added, "I think tonight would be a perfect time."

"What are you up to, big brother?"

He leaned forward with a conspiring look. "I want to give Myla her Christmas present, is all. Oh, and take Shredder with you. I don't want any children, dogs, cats, old girlfriends, or sisters around when I do it."

Myla sat on Henny's bed, reading a how-to book on opening a small business that Lydia had given her for Christmas. A cup of lemon-mint tea steamed nearby, while Shredder snoozed in a curled ball at her feet. Dusk played across the back gardens, coloring them in a golden brilliance that reminded her of the paper Jesse's mermaid doll had been wrapped in. Shaking her head, she wondered if Nick had wrapped it himself, or paid a department store a pretty penny to do the job.

Placing the book on a nearby table, she rose to watch the cold December dusk entice the waning sun behind the trees. It had been a good Christmas, but it was almost over. This would soon only be a memory. Nick would soon be a memory. Would he think about her after she'd moved on with her life?

She sighed, then settled into a wing chair to read some more of her new book. This quiet time was much needed and appreciated. Lydia was such a help with the children and they loved her. They'd miss that attention when they had to leave.

Where was Nick? He'd mysteriously disappeared right after the meal. Was he at Carolyn's house, begging her to understand why he'd been late yet again?

A tapping on the partially opened door caused Myla to glance up. Nick poked his head in, a hesitant smile cresting his features. "May I come in?"

She slapped the book shut, rising up out of the chair to greet him. At the sight of him in a tuxedo with his dark hair glistening, she had to hold her breath. How she envied Carolyn right now.

"Going out?"

He walked into the room, stopping inches from her. "No, I'm dining in tonight."

"But I…after our late dinner, I thought—" She tried to hurry around him. "I'll go warm things up right now."

"Myla, you don't have to rush into the kitchen and cook."

The look in his eyes caught her, holding her

with its secretive warmth. It was a look of knowing, a look of wonderment, a look of pure pleasure.

"Okay. What's going on?"

"We're going to spend some time alone," he explained. "And I've instructed Lydia to take good care of the children, so don't worry."

Wary of his motives, she asked, "Is this some sort of scheme to make up for your extravagance?"

"Are you still mad about that?"

"No, I'm not so mad now."

"Good. I want you to put everything out of your mind. Don't worry about the children, or this house, or the future. Can you do that for a little while, Myla?"

"But Nick—"

"No questions. Trust me."

He reached out a hand, and she took it, the beat of her heart following his lead. Trust. That was the one thing standing between them. She hadn't quite learned how to trust again.

As if sensing her reluctance, Nick smiled down at her. "Come on, Myla. It's Christmas. Let's enjoy it together."

Christmas. A time of love and miracles. Was it so selfish to want a little of the joy for herself?

The sight that greeted her was indeed full of magic.

Nick took her to the glass-enclosed sunroom off the den, where a table was set for two, complete with candlelight and two steaming mugs of hot chocolate. And all around the room were roses, dozens and dozens of yellow roses, sitting amid the scented candles and the ficus trees. She'd never seen so many shades of the color yellow. The fat, buttery petals ranged in shades from pale cream to deep, bright lemon, and the fragrance reminded her of her own long-lost rose garden.

Tears misted her eyes as one word escaped her throat. "How?"

He looked pleased as punch. "My secret. But before we eat, I've got a few other surprises for you."

She couldn't speak. When she held back, he said, "Trust me, remember?"

Then he handed her a basket full of scented soaps and colorful bottles of bubble bath, along with her mug of hot chocolate.

"Thank you," she said, pleased with his thoughtfulness. "It's been a very long time since I've indulged in a bubble bath."

"And this," he added, handing her a large, colorfully wrapped box.

Gushing, she set her other goodies down, then opened the box to find a full-skirted, round-necked dress with long, tight-fitting sleeves. The fabric was a flowing, vivid Christmas green brocade. "Oh, Nick, it's beautiful, but I can't accept this."

"Yes, you can. I want you to go back to your room and enjoy your soaps and bubbles, soak for as long as you want. Then put on your new frock. We'll eat when you're ready."

Surprised, she shook her head. "I can't. The children, the kitchen needs cleaning. I've got a million things to do."

"Not right now. Now, go. I'm still the boss around here, remember?"

She saw the teasing light in his eyes and sighed. "You're spoiling me just as much as you tried to spoil my children."

"Let me, for just a little while?" he asked in a quiet tone. A request, not an order, Myla noticed.

She looked up at him, seeing the need in his eyes. He wanted to do this, needed to be able to give. But this was more than showering her with gifts, this was a gift from his heart. Her own heart answered, beating tightly against her chest.

She turned to go, but stopped at the door to glance back. "How did you know, about the roses?"

He lifted a finger to his lips and smiled. "My secret."

She went into her room and ran a long, bubbly bath and enjoyed reliving each of his gifts. A bubble bath. A new dress. Yellow roses.

Then suddenly it hit her how he'd figured it all out.

The children! Now she knew. Her children had told him her fondest desires. Overcome with joy, she tried not to cry. Not now. Maybe tomorrow, or the next week, when she was alone and struggling again, but not now. But she wouldn't cry tears of pity; her tears would be full of joy for a man who'd tried to make her dreams come true, for a man who'd seemed so distant until he'd touched her, physically and spiritually. A man she'd fallen in love with.

I love him, she thought. Maybe she'd loved him from the first time she'd seen him there on the road. But would she ever be able to admit to that love?

Trust me, he'd said. Could she?

"Just for tonight, Nick," she whispered as she relaxed in the scented bubbles. "Just for tonight."

Chapter Six

A little while later, Myla entered the sunroom with an expectant feeling of hope, her eyes meeting Nick's in shy anticipation.

Nick swallowed hard, then extended his hand, his heart beating against the tucking of his shirt. He'd wanted everything to be perfect, but he'd never dreamed a woman could look so lovely, so radiant. "You look wonderful. The dress becomes you."

She patted her upswept red hair and lowered her head. "You did a great job of guessing my size."

"The children helped out there."

"Ah, would that be the same children who told you about my silly daydreams?"

"The very same. Did I leave anything out?"

She took the glass of mineral water he offered her. "No, not a thing." Then reaching out to touch one of the roses, she said, "Thank you for the flowers. It means a lot to me."

He guided her toward the table. "Well, if I have it my way, you'll never be without yellow roses again."

His firm declaration touched Myla, making her love him even more. "Sonny hated them," she said quietly.

"I could never hate anything that made you happy," he replied steadily. Then, "Hungry?" He lifted the top off a silver server.

Myla relaxed then, bursting out in a fit of laughter. "Turkey sandwiches?"

He grinned. "My specialty. I'm not as proficient in the kitchen as you. I did, however, bring a bag of chips and the rest of the pecan pie."

"Oh, that reminds me," she said, sitting down, "I've got a surprise for you. I'll give it to you after we eat."

Nick helped her with her chair. "I thought I was the one full of surprises."

She watched him sit down. "You certainly are, and I really appreciate all of this."

Reaching out, she took his hand to say grace. "Thank You, for bringing Nick and me together to heal each other. Thank You for finding me a place to feel safe when there was no room in the inn. In the same way You protected Your Son, Jesus Christ, on the night of His birth, I ask You to now protect us on this holiest of holidays. Amen."

Nick looked up at her, his hand still holding hers. "I want to tell you something."

"All right."

"I saw Carolyn on Christmas Eve."

Myla's heart sank. Had he done all of this just to let her down easily? Swallowing her pride, she said, "I know. You don't have to explain."

"Yes, I do. I told her I can't see her anymore. We both knew it wasn't going anywhere. Carolyn has a lot of things she needs to work through, but I'm not the one she needs to make her happy. I'd rather be here, with you."

Myla's eyes brimmed with fresh tears. "Do you mean that?"

"Yes, I certainly do. I understand we also have a lot to deal with, a lot of things to get cleared up between us. But I'm willing to try. I'm willing to work toward that commitment you need."

"Meaning, you're ready to make a commitment to Christ?"

He nodded, then bowed his head. "Yes, I am. But I'll need your help."

"I'll be here."

Lifting his head, he said, "What about Magnolia House? What about finding your own place?"

"I can do all that, and we can still get to know

each other. It can work, Nick. All I ask for is some time."

It wasn't the answer he'd hoped for, but he didn't intend to give up. Not at all. "Okay. I've been told patience is a virtue. Eat your sandwich."

He smiled, content for now to sit and watch the play of candlelight on her face. Later, he'd figure out how to keep her by his side.

Myla smiled back, then lowered her head, the action causing a tendril of hair to slip over her brow in a looping curl.

Nick Rudolph, ruthless oil millionaire and man of action, was left breathless and speechless—immobilized by an endearing smile and a wayward curl.

Myla Howell, the no-nonsense, pragmatic woman, felt like a princess—captivated by a set of golden brown eyes and the scent of yellow roses.

The meal was wonderful, Myla decided. She could see the change in Nick, from the glow in his dark eyes to the sincerity of his smile. And she loved him because he'd been willing to change, for her. Tonight, she refused to think about her doubts or how she'd ever be able to leave this lovely house—and this lovable man.

They finished the meal, then Nick held out his hand to her to dance to the soft Christmas music playing from the stereo. Bing Crosby sang about being home for Christmas.

Confused, Myla sank into his arms. "I...I haven't danced in a very long time."

Nick snuggled closer to her. "You should dance. You should enjoy life to the fullest."

"Sonny didn't like dancing."

He frowned, then spoke into her ear. "Well, I do."

His nearness left her feeling lightweight and listless. Breathless. "You're very good at it, too."

He lifted his head, his gaze slipping over her face like brown velvet. "It helps to have a lovely woman in my arms."

"Nick, I—"

He held a finger to her parted lips. "No doubts. Not tonight, Myla, remember. It's Christmas."

"So it is," she said, her face inches from his, her eyes shining.

He lowered his head to hers, kissing her with all the warmth he felt in his heart. She accepted his touch, his need, as her own. His gentleness moved her beyond doubt.

And so, they danced, slowly, quietly, softly, while the winter wind lifted up to the glowing stars outside.

When the song ended, Myla took him by the hand, pulling him into the kitchen. "Want your surprise now?"

Not wanting the moment to end, Nick held

back. "Hey, I set the rules. Who said you could start bringing out surprises?"

"How about, together we make a new set of rules?"

"Sounds good to me. My father taught me the old set, and I don't think they worked so very good."

"Sit down," she instructed, shoving him into a chair, "and close your eyes."

"I like this game," he teased, his eyes tightly shut.

The smell of pound cake wafted through the warm kitchen. "Ah, now I know this has been the best Christmas ever."

"Okay, open your eyes."

The cake sat whole and fat before him, waiting for him to take the first slice. He didn't remember having ever received a better present.

"You carve, and I'll make coffee," she called over her shoulder.

"Hey, just a minute." He stood up to pull her into his arms. Giving her a thorough kiss, he said, "Merry Christmas, Myla."

"Merry Christmas, Nick."

"Now, let's eat some of that cake before something happens to destroy it!"

Three a.m. Nick stood by the fireplace in his bedroom, watching the dying embers with unseeing eyes.

It had started out innocently enough. All he'd wanted to do was show Myla a good time. Give her something special for Christmas. An evening she'd always remember.

Instead, she'd given him an evening he'd never be able to forget. She'd looked so very beautiful in her new dress that was the exact shade of her exotic green eyes.

Nick had realized two things this Christmas evening. One, he'd been lost in this big house, and he'd been lost in life. He wanted to be found. And two, he had fallen in love with Myla Howell, maybe from the first time he'd seen her. It didn't matter. What did matter was that he loved her and wanted to make a life with her.

Now, he had to be very sure and very careful. Wisely, she'd seen things in him he hadn't even seen himself. He wanted to take care of her, to love her and cherish her. But in order to do that, he might have to make one of the hardest choices in his life. He might have to let her go, in order to gain her love.

And, he'd never been very good at letting go.

Thinking about her need to be independent and self-sufficient, he said a prayer for courage and patience. Then it occurred to him, his father had neglected to teach him the most important rule of all.

Follow your heart.

* * *

Myla groaned, stopping on the busy street corner to rest for a minute, her thoughts rushing by like the lunch-time traffic. The last few days since she, Nick and the children had spent a quiet New Year's Eve together had been busy and tiring. With the new year had come the realization that she needed to hunt for a new job, and prepare herself for the move into Magnolia House. This morning, she'd driven into the city to do just that, but something had happened that had left her shaken and confused, and more determined than ever to improve her standard of living.

Checking the digital clock on a nearby bank building, she reasoned she'd have enough time to meet Lydia and Nick for lunch and make it by Magnolia House to fill out some forms, before it was time for the children to get home from school. Even as she stood there, her empty stomach rumbled an urgent message, and her head felt light from lack of sustenance.

The sign over her head announced the Milam Street Coffeehouse. Lydia had said to meet them here. Pushing the dark-tinted heavy door open, Myla looked up to find a familiar face watching her from the other side.

Nick. He looked as wonderful as the coffee smelled. She didn't know if her stomach lurched from hunger, or from the sight of him waiting there for her. Every bit the successful business tycoon, he was dressed in a dark wool suit and cream-colored shirt, the browns and blues in his tie picking up on his dark good looks.

Myla's heart thudded, causing her next words to rumble much like her empty stomach. "Well, hello there. Where's Lydia?"

Nick grinned, then stood to greet her. "She got tied up with a phone call. Sent me on ahead to meet you." Glancing around with disapproval, he added, "Although this place wouldn't have been my first choice." Guiding her to a chair, he said, "You look tired."

She couldn't yet bring herself to tell him what had happened to her today, so she just said, "Job hunting is hard work."

He waved to a nearby waiter. "You'll feel better after you eat something. And, I have a bit of good news, I think."

"Oh, and what's that?"

"Lydia said something about knowing the man who owns this restaurant. He's looking for help, and that's why she wanted you to meet us here."

Myla glanced around at the eclectic style of the new eatery, her eyes scanning the paintings by local artists and the other forms of artwork decorating the two-storied open-air building. "It's different, but I like it."

Nick didn't look so sure. "Well, I don't. This

place doesn't look as classy as Lydia described. Hope the food is good, at least."

"Hope I get hired," Myla said in a weary voice.

Nick didn't like the idea of her working in an eclectic restaurant centered in a run-down building, but he didn't think she'd listen to him. "Are you interested?"

Her eyes lit up. "Of course. I got really down this morning, kind of depressed." Shrugging, she decided not to tell him just how down she'd been. "But I'm better now."

"Good." Taking her hand, Nick waited while she told the waiter she'd have a chicken salad sandwich, then he reluctantly ordered himself a hamburger. "You know, even though Henny's due back any day now, you don't have to move out immediately, and you don't have to take the first job that comes along."

"Thanks," she said, taking a sip of much-needed coffee. Her empty stomach rejected it, though, so she pushed it away. "But I don't want to miss my spot on the list at Magnolia House. It's hard to get in, with so many people needing temporary shelter."

He tapped his fingers on the glass-topped bistro table. "Well, don't overdo things. Lydia tells me you've already enrolled in a business class and a cake-decorating course for the spring."

"Yes, I need both to get me started and give me some experience."

Finally, his patience sorely tried, Nick said, "Look, you don't have to move into the shelter at all. I have guest rooms. You can stay as long as you want."

Both hands on her coffee cup, Myla said, "Nick, we agreed that I'd leave after Christmas. I'm not your responsibility, and technically, it wouldn't be right."

"But I feel responsible…I want to be responsible for you, and technically, we wouldn't be doing anything wrong. I'd be a perfect gentleman."

Touched by his thoughtfulness, she said, "That means a lot to me, because I know you are a gentleman, and if I get in a pinch, I'll call you. But I need this time, if for nothing else, to prove to myself that I'm capable. I depended on Sonny for so much…it's time I learned how to deal with things on my own."

He ran a hand through his hair, frustrated with her stubborn determination. "Yes, and I promised I'd give you some time to do just that. I'm sorry."

Sitting back in her chair, she said, "I'm going to Magnolia House after we eat. You're welcome to come along and see the place for yourself."

"I just might," he replied. "Lydia's been after

me to take a tour ever since the place opened. Of course, I'll probably take one look at it and tell you not to leave me."

The way he'd said that spoke much more than mere words. They sat looking at each other for a minute, then Myla said, "I'm not leaving you, Nick. I'm just doing what I have to do. We can still see each other."

"Right. You think you have to do this, to prove something to yourself and the world. I'm trying very hard to accept that and understand."

"And I appreciate your efforts. If we still… feel the same about our relationship after a few months, we'll see what happens next."

He continued tapping on the glass tabletop. "I know, I know. Patience is a virtue."

She shot him a broad smile. "Hebrews, chapter 10, verse 36—'For ye have need of patience, that, after ye have done the will of God, ye might receive the promise.'"

Nick shook his head. "That's all great, but what about my will?"

"You have to give that over to Him, for now."

"It's hard."

"But you'll receive the promise."

"Which is?"

"A good life, the life you desire."

When she looked up, Nick's eyes were centered on her. "I hope the life I desire turns out to be with you."

His reply overwhelmed her. What was he saying? Had he really come to care for her as much as she cared for him? Afraid she'd cave in, she asked, "Have you heard from Henny?"

He leaned back in his chair to loosen his tie a notch. "Only to say she'd be here any day now. She sounded odd, not herself, kind of distant and tired. I'm worried about her," he added with concern. "Her health isn't good at all these days but she's far too stubborn to let anyone know if she's not feeling well."

"Maybe she misses fussing over you. And me, I've got to continue this job search. I'll talk to the owner here, to see what he has to offer, then fill out a few more applications."

Nick did not want her to work in this fledgling establishment. It was just like Lydia to go for the underdog, even in her choice of restaurants, but that didn't mean Myla had to work here.

"Can you type?" he asked, his tone light and hopeful.

"Barely. I haven't since high school."

"I don't suppose you've ever worked on an oil rig?"

Myla looked skeptical until she saw the laugh crinkles surrounding his eyes. "No, but thanks for the offer. So far, I've been turned away at six restaurants, two offices, three fast-food joints, and a half-dozen retail stores. I've offered to cook, clean, type and file, and just about anything else I can think of. The job market is slim for a woman without a college degree who's fast approaching her thirties. But I'm not the only one." She looked down at the marble design on their table. "Today, I saw several people worse off than me."

Nick stopped his tapping. "I can't imagine not having a job. My grandfather did all the scraping and clawing in my family."

His words reminded Myla of Sonny. "You know, Sonny's parents gave him everything. They spoiled him, then when he got out on his own, he couldn't handle the responsibility." She glanced up at Nick, a deep sorrow filling her soul. "Money really can't solve our problems, no matter how much we think it can. So just be glad you've done a good, honest job of holding on to what your grandfather built."

He looked sheepish. "I'm not so proud. I'm an overachiever, and unlike Sonny, I am responsible—my parents taught both of us that lesson—and a lot of people depend on me."

Myla knew he was right there. Nick had a strong sense of responsibility. And now, he had taken her on as his own responsibility, too. "Does it get to you, knowing people's livelihoods depend on your daily decisions?"

"Sometimes, yes, but I've never had time to dwell on it too much. My father had bad timing." A dark look twisted his features. "He died right in the middle of the oil crisis, and I've been trying to keep my head above water ever since. So far, I've done a passable job…Rudolph Oil is still intact."

"But what about its leader? It's important to take care of your spiritual side, too." Sensing his need to talk, she said, "Tell me about your father."

Running a finger over his coffee mug, Nick looked away. "He died of a broken heart. He loved his company and my mother. Watching her die from cancer wasn't easy for any of us, and then when he thought he was going to lose Rudolph Oil, too…" He shrugged, then turned quiet again.

Myla saw him in a new light, understanding why he'd tried so hard to stay detached and distant. Pain did that to people. Touching his hand, she said, "Haven't you done enough scraping and clawing yourself? You do work hard, but you need to work on that chip on your shoulder, too."

"I can't be weak," he said, telling her his worst fear. "I can't become the man my father became. You talk about living a sham—he did.

He thought he was so in control, then he crumbled right before my eyes. I can't let that happen to me."

"God won't let that happen, Nick. Not if you use Him as your strength and your guidance. He won't leave you. If you crumble, He will be there to catch you."

"Maybe. That still doesn't explain my mother's death and my father's heartbreak."

Now she understood completely. He blamed God for making his life miserable. "No, God didn't want you or your parents to suffer. But he can't stop a person from dying when that person's time has come. Sure, the circumstances aren't always pleasant, but that's part of life. God is our guide, but it's up to us to make the first steps toward our journey. That's called free will."

"Free will. The will to make our own choices. But you just quoted me scripture about doing God's will."

"God's will, yes, but based on the right choices," she explained. "We can't blame God for all the bad, and then turn around and expect Him to take care of all the good we want in life. We have to trust in Him, pray for His guidance, then go out and make our own choices, based on an educated, gospel-backed decision. We use the scriptures, past traditions, our own experiences, and our own reasoning, to decide what to do.

And sometimes, we have to face great grief and bitter sadness, but we go on, using God's love as our strength."

All around them, the restaurant flowed and ebbed with people. The sound of the cash register computing tabs blended with the burr of a coffee grinder, while the laughter and whispered words of the few patrons filtered up to the high ceilings.

"Life goes on," Nick said, his gaze settling on hers. "How'd you get to be so wise?"

"Not me, the Bible," she replied, hoping she'd helped him feel better about things. And herself as well.

Just then a tall man with sandy blond hair and horn-rimmed glasses brought their food to the table. Nick immediately gave the grinning man a get-lost look.

But the lanky man continued to stare. "Hey, I'm Grant Lewis. I own this place. Lydia told me to look for you today—she described a tall woman with long red hair and uh...an uptight executive."

Myla giggled while Nick frowned. "That's us," she said.

Nick had no choice but to shake the man's hand, then watch with jealous politeness as Grant smiled down on Myla.

"So, this must be the great cook Lydia's been hounding me to hire."

Myla shook his hand, then asked, "Do you need someone?"

"Sure do," Grant replied as he pushed at his glasses, his blue eyes bright with hope. "One of my best waitresses quit last week. She's a college student and her course load was too heavy. Said she had to crack the books or lose her scholarship."

Myla nodded her understanding, then said, "Well, I can start right away, but only part-time for now."

Nick shot her a warning look. "Don't be so hasty. You don't even know what he's paying."

"Minimum wage plus tips," Grant replied, his hands on his hips. "We're not in the black yet, but we're getting there, so hopefully I'll be able to offer you better pay one day."

"One day? She needs a stable job right now," Nick said, his scowl deepening. "And she has one, with me."

Myla watched Nick's brow furrow. So much for being patient. "Nick, I need a *permanent* job," she reminded him gently.

Grant obviously hadn't missed the friction between them. "Is there a problem?"

"Yes," Nick retorted.

"No," Myla insisted. Giving Nick a meaningful glare, she added, "Mr. Rudolph is afraid of letting me make my own choices, but I'd be happy to work for you, Grant. After all, we did agree that I'd need to find another job soon, right, Nick?"

Nick shrugged, frowned, then sighed long and hard. Just to show Grant that he wasn't as uptight as his sister had implied, he said, "Oh, all right. It's your decision."

Myla smiled appreciatively. "I can start today, if you need me. But until I can find adequate child care, I can only work the early shifts—I have two children. And right now, I have to fill in for Nick's housekeeper, but she's due home any day now."

Grant waved both arms. "That sure would help. As you can see, we stay pretty busy with the lunch crowd. Lydia tells me you can cook, but do you have a problem with waiting tables?"

"No, of course not," Myla replied. "I'll do whatever needs to be done. I really need a job. I'll be moving into Magnolia House in a few days."

Grant adjusted the salt and pepper shakers, then shook her hand again. "Lydia explained your situation, and I understand completely. When you're done with your meal, come to the counter and fill out some paperwork. I've got to get back to the kitchen."

After Grant left, Myla looked over at Nick. He didn't look as happy about this as she felt. Wanting reassurance, and wanting him to know that she appreciated his help, she said, "What do you think?"

"I think I'm going to be very jealous of Grant Lewis," he admitted. "You'll be working closely with him every day."

"Nick—that's very flattering, but I'll be fine. I only have eyes for men who buy me yellow roses."

That made him smile. "I'll keep you in a fresh supply to remind you—and him."

Lydia fluttered onto a chair just then, collapsing in an elegant pile against the table. "Nourishment, please?"

Grant was back, Nick noticed. Johnny on the spot.

"Hey, Lydia." Grant said, beaming like a street lamp.

There went that puppy-dog grin again.

"Grant!" Lydia sat straight up, causing her silk floral print scarf to do a fast float. "Nice to see you again." Smiling over at her brother and Myla, she said, "Did Grant tell you he writes poetry? He's a very good writer," she added emphatically.

Grant looked sheepish, then lifted a hand in explanation. "We have open-mike night sometimes. People can share their work."

Not liking the way Grant was ogling his sister, Nick said, "How very generous of you."

Myla caught Nick's blazing gaze, her look

warning him to back off. It was obvious Grant was smitten with Lydia. And vice versa.

Leaning close while Grant and Lydia flirted tactfully with each other, she said, "Well, at least you don't have to be jealous of Grant with *me*. Not with Lydia around."

Nick glared at the man who'd just ruined his day completely. "No, I just have to worry about some smooth-talking artistic type hoodwinking my baby sister."

"He's not trying to hoodwink anybody," Myla whispered as Lydia's sharp ears perked up. "Now, be nice."

"I don't want to be nice. And I intend to have a private conversation with Lydia later. She's far too gullible and naive when it comes to these matters." Concentrating on Myla again, he said, "You haven't eaten much."

Myla's stomach did a revolt as she eyed her half-eaten sandwich. "I guess I'm too keyed up to eat." She stood up, turning to Grant. "Could you give me that application? I can fill it out while we finish."

Grant managed to tear his eyes away from Lydia. "Sure, just come on back to the kitchen." Then to Lydia he said, "Stay here. I'll be right back."

Whirling around, Myla started to follow Grant.

The room began to spin, making her feel as if she were being sucked into a huge black vortex.

"Myla?" Nick saw her go pale, watched as she stumbled, then crumpled into a heap. He reached out to catch her as she went limp.

Grant came rushing over to pull her chair out, while Lydia took her hand. "She doesn't look too great," he said, his eyes meeting Nick's.

"Myla, can you hear me?" Nick asked softly, concern evident in his words. "What's wrong?"

"Blood," she managed to whisper.

"Blood?" Nick looked down, searching for any signs of red. "Did you hurt yourself?"

She raised an arm to show him the wide bandage running across the fold inside her elbow joint. "I gave blood this morning. It always makes me queasy."

Lydia's worried gaze flew to Nick's face. "We need to get her home."

Grant took her arm, then shook his head. "Ah, man, they do it all the time."

"Do what?" Nick screamed, all sorts of horrible thoughts rushing through his head.

"Homeless people," Grant explained. "They give plasma to get money. It doesn't pay much, but when you're out of work, it will buy food."

Shocked, Nick looked down at the woman in his arms. "Myla, do you need money that badly?"

Slowly, Myla opened her eyes to focus on his

face. "No, I don't need money too much now, thanks to you. But…someone I met today did. So I gave some blood. I had to do it, Nick. Please try to understand."

Chapter Seven

"You're right, Lydia. I don't understand."

Nick paced the length of the kitchen, his eyes dark with a rage he couldn't even begin to contain. "Giving plasma for money! I've never heard of such a thing. I give blood...I donate regularly at the Red Cross, but she did it out of some sort of desperation. And she didn't even take the time to eat properly before or after she did it. She's barely above the required weight, to begin with!"

"Nick, calm down," Lydia said, her gaze shifting to the array of voices coming from the den. "Myla will be back in here soon. It won't do for her to see you so upset."

"Oh, she knows I'm upset."

He glanced toward the den where Jesse and Patrick were playing with Shredder and their Christmas toys. Myla was in Henny's room, washing her face.

"Yes, I imagine she does, since you practically carried her all the way to your car—after causing a scene with your ranting. Thank goodness Grant was able to stay calm, at least."

Pulling his hands through his hair, Nick grimaced. Now he was being compared to a poet! "Yes, Grant Lewis is a very understanding man. He did settle me down. And he got Myla to nibble on a cracker and drink some juice."

Lydia smiled slightly, relief washing over her youthful face. "Yeah, Grant is so sweet. I've gotten to know him better since approaching him about this job for Myla. In fact, we have a date tonight."

Nick looked at his little sister as if she'd lost her head. "A date? You hardly know the man!"

"I'm getting to know him," Lydia stated. "And don't you start with me. You never approve of anybody I date."

Nick cringed at that accusation. "That's not true. I liked Ralph Pimperton."

"Ralph Pimperton is a pompous…snob."

"Well, yes, he is that, but he really liked you, and he comes from a fine family."

"I didn't like *him,* Nick. Now, please promise me you won't try to intimidate Grant. He's really shy, you know."

Nick glowered at her. "This day is going from bad to worse. First Myla takes a job that I think is unsuitable, then she faints, and now you're telling me you're smitten with a coffeehouse poet."

Lydia stood nose to nose with her brother. "He's more than that. He's a good, decent man and I'm glad to know him. And his place of business is very suitable."

Nick gave his sister a quizzical look, his protective instincts surfacing all over again. "Well, get to know him even a little more before you get all mushy about him."

Lydia stuck her tongue out at him, contradicting her words. "I'm a grown woman, Nick. I know how to handle my own social life, thank you very much. And Myla knows how to find a job. You'd better just stay out of all of this."

Heaving a heavy sigh, Nick tried to relax a little as he listened to the noise coming from the den. He didn't like having to second-guess women. He did, however, like the noise that children could make, he decided. He especially liked knowing they were all here, safe and happy. And he guessed his sister deserved to be happy, too. But what was so wrong with wanting to protect the people he cared about?

But Lydia was right. He couldn't control her life forever. And he certainly couldn't control Myla's, not when he'd promised her he wouldn't interfere.

"Oh, all right. Invite him over for dinner sometime," he suggested, defeat pulling him down. "That way, *I* can get to know him, too."

Lydia grabbed him by the head, then gave him a wet, sisterly kiss. "That's the spirit. I think you'll be pleasantly surprised."

"Well, I've had enough surprises for one day," he said in a low growl.

The sound of a door shutting brought his head up. Myla came in, her walk not nearly as wobbly as it'd been earlier. Nick gave his sister an imploring look.

"I'll go play with the other kids," Lydia said, winking at her brother.

Nick shot her a mock nasty glare, then turned to the auburn-haired woman who'd caused him no small amount of worry, and joy, over the last few weeks. "Are you all right?"

"Much better," she said quietly. "I'll start dinner."

He reached out a hand to stop her. "Forget dinner. Lydia's taking care of that. We need to talk."

Myla placed both hands on the sparkling clean counter, avoiding the accusation in his eyes. She really didn't want to talk about her reasons for doing what she'd done. In spite of her calm front, she was still shaken.

Nick stood across from her, his own hands braced tightly against the same counter. "Myla, if you need more money—"

"I don't. That's not why I gave the plasma."

"Then, please, explain it to me."

She brought her hands together, then clasped them in front of her, closing her eyes for a minute. "I was out job hunting, walking the streets from door to door, and I passed a plasma center. I was tired, worried, frustrated, and there was this line of people blocking my way. Then I saw the sign that said the center would pay for plasma. I looked around at the people—they were waiting to give blood."

She stopped, taking a long swallow as tears welled in her eyes. "That's when I saw this old man, dressed in ragged clothes, sitting on the curb. He looked so gaunt and frail, and when he saw me coming, he held up a hand and asked me if I had a few dollars so he could buy food. He explained that he wanted to give plasma, to get some money. But he wasn't in very good shape. The nurses had turned him away."

She looked up at Nick, her expression grim. "So I offered to go in and give my own plasma. When I came out, I gave him the fifteen dollars I'd earned. It upset me so badly, I gave him the money, then I ran away, down the street." Lowering her head, she covered her face with both hands. "I didn't want to wind up like that, but I had this horrible vision of my children standing in the street begging for food. I sat on a bench and…after a few minutes, I was okay. Just a moment of self-pity. I was so ashamed of how I'd reacted, I tried to forget all about it. But I can't get that old man's face out of my mind."

She looked up, seeing the compassion in Nick's eyes, hoping he could understand how profound seeing the homeless man had been for her, that she'd had no choice but to help him in some way.

"Myla." He came around the counter to take her in his arms. "You're not so very tough, after all, are you?"

Myla leaned against him, allowing herself this simple luxury. "No, I'm not tough. I'm scared to death of being a failure. I can't let my children down, though."

Nick patted her back, then lifted her chin so he could see her face. "You won't let them down. I know that in my heart. What you did was a sweet and noble thing, but you don't have to worry. I won't allow that to happen to you and your children."

"But what about that old man? What about all the children lost out there in the cold and the dark? Somebody has to do something. We can't just keep running away from people who need our help."

He couldn't answer that. "I know they're out there. And we can try to help, but we can't save all of them."

She looked up then, a new light of hope cresting in her eyes. "But you will help me, right? You'll help me to find a way to save some of these people. I have to do it, Nick. I know how they feel."

A strange thudding began deep inside Nick's chest. Was this his calling then, to help those who couldn't help themselves? Was this a way to bring him closer to God, and his beloved Myla? Was this a way to redeem himself at last?

"We'll do it," he said. "Whatever we can, we'll do it, together. I promise."

Myla hugged him close, a new warmth flowing through her tired body. "That was worth fainting over," she said, her worry turning to happiness.

He stroked her hair, then said, "Well, just promise me you'll take care of yourself. You gave me a bad scare back there."

"I'll be fine now."

The back doorbell rang, bringing Patrick bounding through the kitchen. "Pizza man's here. He sure got here quick."

Nick took Myla by the hand to head for the door. "He knows the address well," he said dryly.

"Another week." Myla's attention shifted from Nick's worried expression to Lydia's pleased one. "I'm next on the list. I can move into Magnolia

House this weekend. With my new job, and now this, my life is beginning to take shape again. I won't have to resort to welfare."

Nick wished he could be as happy about this as the two women sitting across from him in his kitchen. Lydia was positively giddy over the poet fellow, the noble Mr. Grant Lewis, and now Myla was happily working two jobs and in sheer joy about moving into a homeless shelter, of all places. He really, truly, would never understand women.

Glancing up from his apple strudel, he gave Myla an encouraging look in spite of his mixed feelings about her leaving. "How long will you be able to stay there?"

Seeing the worry in his eyes, she tried to reassure him. "We can stay up to a year, but I don't intend to let it drag out that long. I'm saving as much money as I can to find a low-rent place."

Still concerned, Nick said, "Now explain how this place works to me again. I want to understand the whole process."

Lydia piped up. "I've been explaining it to you, but you never listen." At her brother's wince of disapproval, she said, "Grant was interested, so I gave him a tour. He's more than willing to help out with the homeless situation in this city."

"Very honorable," Nick said. "Is there anything the wonderful Grant Lewis isn't willing to do for you—or to you—for that matter?"

"Nick!" Hurt, Lydia implored Myla. "Will you please ask my overbearing brother if he could possibly put a little faith and trust in me."

Myla glanced at Nick, her brows lifting in a question. When Nick only pouted, she said, "Look, I work with Grant every day. He's a very nice man."

"His company isn't very stable," Nick argued. "The restaurant business is fickle and unpredictable. He might have to shut down any day now."

"You know that for a fact?" Lydia asked, anger slicing through her words.

Nick looked smug. "No, but I know enough about business to predict such things."

"We're getting rave reviews," Myla stated. "In fact...Grant and I are considering opening up a catering business just as soon as I can get back on my feet."

"What?" Nick gave her a surprised look. "Myla, don't overextend yourself."

"I won't," she said, a wary tone in her words. "Grant's already allowed me to do some extra cooking. We're trying out new recipes on the customers. And just as soon as Henny's able to come back to work, I intend to expand on that."

Nick threw up his hands. "Can we concentrate on one change at a time? Let's get back to talking about Magnolia House. If I hear one more word of praise for Grant Lewis, I think I'll lose my lunch."

"Poor Nick, he never handled change very well," Lydia explained to Myla, before launching into a thorough speech on how the homeless shelter was set up. "Magnolia House is a transitional place, not just a homeless shelter. It's more like an apartment building, and since this is a new program to help the homeless, it's in high demand. It's always full—a sign that this problem is growing."

Myla offered Nick some more strudel, hoping to soothe his temper and his concern, but put the lid back on the pan when he silently refused with a shake of his head. Taking a bite of her own dessert, she said, "Which is why I'm anxious to learn all I can about it and help others."

"We're behind you all the way. Grant's willing to help and we know big brother wants in on the action. Right, Nick?" Lydia gave her brooding brother a hearty shake.

Nick moaned, then sighed long and hard before glancing over at Myla. "Don't you just love eternally perky people?"

Myla gave him a serious glance. "Do you want to help us with this, or not?"

Turning serious himself, he nodded. "Absolutely. I'm already looking into it. I've talked to several other prominent businessmen in the area, and they've pledged their support, too."

"Thank you." Myla started clearing the dessert dishes away. "I'll bring home some more information next time I go in."

The phone rang nearby, and Lydia hopped up to get it, giving Nick an opportunity to talk to Myla alone. "I guess this is it, then. You'll be leaving soon."

"Yes," she said, her heart fluttering at the thought of having to leave the safety of this wonderful old house. "I don't want you to worry about me, though. I'm tough and I have a strong sense that this is what the Lord wants me to do."

Nick wanted to tell her he had his own strong sense about what she needed to do, but he held back. "You and my baby sister," he said, shaking his head in wonder. "You both seem so sure, so confident. Me, I'm still floundering around, afraid."

Myla smiled at his endearing self-doubt. "Lydia will be all right, Nick. Grant is really a decent man."

Nick nodded, his eyes on his sister. "I guess I hadn't realized she's all grown-up."

"And very capable of taking care of herself," Myla reminded him. "You should be very proud of her."

Lydia's concerned call to Nick stopped his reply.

"It's Henny's daughter. They had to rush Henny to the hospital. Nick, they think it's her heart."

Myla heard the fear in Lydia's voice and saw that same fear shooting through Nick's dark eyes. She listened as Nick took the phone, then placed her arm around Lydia's shaking shoulders.

"I see," he said into the receiver. "Keep us posted. Call day or night, collect. And we'll be on the first plane up there—I don't care what Henny says—I'm coming."

Hanging up the phone, he turned in shock to his sister. She fell into his arms, her muffled cries absorbed into his shirt.

"It'll be okay, honey," he said, kissing Lydia's fluffy bob. "We'll go up there to be with her, make sure she takes care of herself." He looked over her head at Myla, his expression dark and grim.

The pain Myla saw in his eyes ripped her heart apart. She'd seen Nick struggle to downplay his emotions, but this pain was too fresh and too much of a shock to hide.

"Nick, what can I do?" she asked, wanting to comfort him.

Gently extracting Lydia from his arms, Nick handed his sister a tissue.

Lydia rushed away, a new batch of tears welling in her usually bright eyes. "I'll go call the airline and book us a flight."

Nick waited until his sister had left the room, then turned back to Myla. "Lydia's been warning me about Henny's health. But I was always too busy, too absorbed in myself, to notice."

Myla knew he was telling the truth. And she also knew he'd changed a great deal in the last month. She watched as he tried to shut himself down, as he struggled against the old pains and resentments. Giving him some time alone, she began clearing the dinner dishes away, but Nick's hand on her arm stopped her.

With a gentle tug, he pulled her close, burying his face against her hair. "Stay. Stay here. I need you to be here when I get back, in case..."

He left the statement hanging, but Myla understood what he was asking. If she stayed, though, she'd risk losing her spot at Magnolia House and a chance at a fresh start. But she knew in her heart she couldn't desert him now.

"Of course I'll stay, Nick. Henny might need help once she gets back."

He lifted his head then, to look into her eyes. "If she doesn't make it back—"

"We have to pray that that doesn't happen,"

she gently reminded him. "But if it does, we'll get through it, together."

"Together," he repeated, his eyes dark and somber. "God sent you to me just in time, didn't He, Myla?"

She patted his cheek. "Go check on your sister."

A few days later, Myla answered the phone at the coffeehouse, expecting it to be an order for a late lunch.

"Myla?"

Nick's voice cut across her midafternoon tiredness, making her snap to attention. She'd been waiting to hear about Henny's condition since Nick and Lydia had left for Little Rock. "Nick, how is she?"

"She made it through the bypass surgery," he said over the wire, his tone hopeful. "The doctors assure us she'll have a full recovery."

Relief flooded through Myla. "That's wonderful. When will she be able to come home?"

He hesitated, then plunged right in. "That's the other reason I'm calling. Her daughter wants her to recuperate here in Little Rock, with her family and the doctors nearby."

"Well, that's understandable." She waited as silence echoed through the line. "Do you want me to stay awhile longer, to help out?"

He let out a long sigh. "You know I'd like nothing better than that, but you'll lose your spot on the list at Magnolia House. I can't ask you to do that, but on the other hand, there's really no need for you to rush now."

Giving up her place at the shelter wouldn't be half as hard if it didn't involve living under the same roof with him, she reasoned. Sending up a prayer for strength and guidance, she swallowed back her concerns. She could do this. She had to do it, for Henny's sake, and to show Nick that she believed in him. She wouldn't run out on him when he needed her the most.

"I'll be here, Nick."

That simple statement seemed to reassure him. "Thank you. I know how much I'm asking, Myla, but I won't forget this. I'll make it up to you, somehow."

Hanging up, Myla looked up from the order pad she'd been doodling on to find Carolyn Parker coming toward her. What on earth was the tall blonde doing here? And why now, of all times, when Myla's doubts were foaming over like the cappuccino she watched Grant mix for a customer.

"Hello," Carolyn said as she dropped down on a stool at the long lunch counter. "How are you, Myla?"

Myla didn't like the appraising look the other

woman was giving her, but she managed a polite smile. "I'm fine. It's good to see you again, Carolyn. I'm sorry about what happened with my children and the cat."

"No problem." Carolyn tossed her long hair away from her face and placed her black leather purse on the counter in front of her. "Guess you're wondering what I'm doing here."

"Well, yes, I am," Myla admitted. "Would you like something to drink?"

"Oh, no. I just wanted to talk to you, about Nick."

"I see."

Carolyn's luminous eyes softened then. "He's changed so much, I guess I'm just trying to understand what's happened to him."

Confused, Myla studied the other woman's face. She looked sincere, and sad. "I don't know if I can help you out, Carolyn. I don't understand Nick too well myself."

"Oh, but you do," Carolyn insisted. "He's different since he met you. And I've been stewing about it for weeks now. You see, I had this silly idea that Nick would ask me to marry him. We've been kind of dating for so long, but I guess in my heart I knew it was more of a convenience than anything else. Still, I never gave up. Until you came along."

"I'm sorry," Myla said, embarrassed at the

woman's directness. "I didn't mean to come between you and Nick."

"Maybe not," Carolyn replied, her eyes cool. "But I can't compete with you and your Bible."

That statement left Myla unsettled. She didn't like the implications of the other woman's words. "What do you mean?"

"I mean, I've seen a lot of come-on lines in my time, but spouting Bible verses is a new one. You have Nick's attention now, but I don't know if you can hold him with that demure little self-righteous act for long."

Shocked, Myla lifted her chin, then gave Carolyn a direct look. "It's not an act. My beliefs are sincere, but I'd never use them to try to win a man. I care about Nick because he took the time to care about me. Maybe you never got any closer to him because you can't see beyond his money or his status."

Carolyn snorted. "And you can?"

Myla bristled, but stood her ground. "Yes, I've seen Nick's gentle side, his caring, giving side. He's a good man, and I'm glad he's changing for the better. You should be, too."

Carolyn rose, her eyes now full of hostility. "Not if it means I have to give him up."

Myla felt sorry for the beautiful blonde. "Maybe you never really had him to begin with."

That caused Carolyn to pause. "Maybe not.

But it's not over yet. You're just a housekeeper, after all. He feels sorry for you. He'll get tired of playing this new game and he'll come back to me. He always does."

Hiding the pain of the put-down and Carolyn's smug assumption behind a serene smile, Myla could only hope that didn't happen. But she wouldn't give Carolyn the satisfaction of seeing her doubt. "If you really love Nick," she said as Carolyn turned to leave, "you'll be glad that he's finally getting over his bitterness and pain. Or were you even aware that he's been suffering all these years?"

Carolyn rolled her eyes and laughed. "Funny, he always seemed happy when he was with me."

"Then you really don't know him at all," Myla said softly.

Carolyn lifted her arched brows. "I know him well enough to warn him away from you. You're living in his house. How does that fit in with your holier-than-thou attitude? Or had you stopped to think what any hint of scandal could do to Nick's reputation and his business?"

With that, Carolyn lowered her head and walked out the door, leaving Myla blushing and angry.

Grant came to stand beside Myla, his eyes on the woman leaving the restaurant. "Wow, who was that?"

"A friend of Nick's," Myla said absently, trying to hide the embarrassment Carolyn's words had inflicted. "And a very lonely woman, apparently."

"That's a shame," Grant replied, his mind already back on business as he greeted a customer across the room.

"Yes, it certainly is," Myla said to herself, her own doubts working their way through her mind in the same steady pace as the lunch crowd had worked its way through the diner earlier. "She's worried about competing with me, but I know I don't stand a chance against her. Especially if she decides to make trouble for Nick."

Just one more thing to add to her list of worries.

Grant came back then. Tapping Myla on the arm, he said, "Hey, where'd you go?"

"Sorry, boss. Just woolgathering. Did you need to talk to me?"

Grant lowered his head, his shy eyes studying the counter. "About our catering business—"

"Don't tell me you've changed your mind?"

"Oh, no." He shook his head. "I want to start it, right away. It will mean lots of long hours, though."

"I can handle it."

"What about your children?"

Myla traced an invisible pattern on the rich

mahogany of the counter. "Well, Lydia has offered to help out. And once I move into Magnolia House, I'll have trained counselors there to help with the children."

"A built-in day care?"

"Something like that." She swallowed the dread back. "I don't have much choice. I have to work. And, I am very interested in this, Grant."

"Enough to form a partnership?"

Surprised, Myla looked over at him, her smile beaming. "Partners? I just thought I'd be working for you."

"I think partners would be better," Grant said. "You have a lot of fresh ideas, and hey, the customers keep coming back for your muffins and cookies."

"They seem to like them," she agreed. Extending a hand to him, she said, "Thank you, Grant. This is like a dream come true."

"Well, don't get too dreamy," he replied. "First, we have to work out a plan and set some goals."

"I'm ready," Myla said. Somehow, she'd make it all work. For her children's sake. She had to remember that their needs would always come first. Even if that meant giving up being with Nick.

Myla's new routine kept her busy, which kept her mind off Carolyn's dire warnings about Nick.

She worked the breakfast and lunch shifts at the coffeehouse, then rushed home to do her work at the mansion while waiting for the children to come home on the school bus. She was tired, but content. With two jobs, she was steadily saving money. Of course, when Henny recovered, one of her jobs would end.

Myla was almost glad Nick had been called away. It would be much easier to leave his home, to leave him, now that she'd had a few days without him in her life. But he was never far from her thoughts. She'd missed him terribly.

Right now, she remembered Nick's knock on her door late last night when he and Lydia returned from Little Rock. He didn't say a whole lot, but she could tell he needed to see a friendly face.

"Thank you for staying," he whispered so as not to wake the sleeping children. With that, he gave her a quick hug before heading upstairs with his tired sister. This morning, he was up and gone before she could get breakfast started. So she came to work wondering if he was really all right, and wondering if he was having second thoughts about their budding relationship.

Just to keep herself busy, she'd baked a blueberry cobbler, and smiling, was happily serving it up to the few customers who'd come in for a late lunch.

"I'll have a double helping, if you don't mind," a deep male voice said into her ear.

Whirling, Myla laughed, her heart skipping a beat as Nick grinned down at her.

"Nick! It's good to have you home."

"It's good to be home," he said, settling onto a bar stool, his expression as carefree as a schoolboy's. "We got back so late last night, we didn't really get a chance to talk. I missed you."

"I missed you, too. How's Henny?"

He took the cobbler Myla automatically scooped up for him, his eyes lighting up at the sight of it. "Doing great. She insisted I come back to check on you. She thinks we were made for each other."

"Were we?"

"I'm beginning to believe that, yes."

Remembering Carolyn's declaration that Nick would soon get bored with her, Myla turned away to finish filling the sugar containers. The sooner she could move out of his house, the better, no matter how much she cared about him. Then she'd be able to think this through and get a clear grasp on reality.

Nick stopped nibbling his cobbler, his eyes locking with hers in the mirror behind the counter. "What's wrong?"

Should she tell him? Deciding to keep things

light, she only said, "I saw Carolyn the other day."

That got his attention. "Really. I haven't talked to her in a while. How's she doing?"

"She seemed confused," Myla admitted. "I think she misses you, too."

"Did she say something to you, to upset you?"

Because she cared for him, she didn't tell him about Carolyn's other threats. "No, not really. Nothing I can't deal with. Maybe you should check on her, though."

Giving her a curious look, he said, "All right. But I have to admit, I'm not accustomed to the woman in my life telling me to call my ex-girlfriend."

"I'm not like other women," she told him in a curt little tone.

"No, you're not. For one thing, you make such an incredible blueberry cobbler, that it makes me want to weep with sheer joy."

She smiled in spite of herself.

He leaned over the counter, his hand touching her face. "And for another, you're much too smart to let anything my ex-girlfriend might say upset you. Right?"

"Right," she said, touched that he'd worded it in a way that didn't force her to admit to anything. "Just see about her for me, all right?"

"All right."

She sat down beside him to drink a quick cup of coffee while he finished his dessert. When he rose to leave, she said, "I'll see you at dinner. I've got a meat loaf ready to pop in the oven."

"Okay." He headed toward the door, thinking how comforting it was to have someone to come home to. He'd rounded the corner, heading the short distance back to Rudolph Oil when Myla's frantic call stopped him.

"Nick!"

Myla's shouts echoed through the skyscrapers. Nick pivoted to find her running toward him, a look of panic draining the color from her face. Hurrying to meet her, he said, "What's the matter?"

"It's Jesse. Her school called. She's got a fever and she's having trouble breathing. I've got to go and get her, but Grant borrowed my car to make a delivery. Can you give me a lift?"

"Of course." Taking her by the arm, he guided her across Milam Street. "My car's parked at the office. It's just around the corner."

"Good. I got one of the other waitresses to cover for me. I really appreciate this. I know you've got a lot of work to catch up on."

"Don't worry about that. I don't mind. I'll call the office from the car and let my secretary know I won't be back today."

They reached his car in record time. As Nick

leaned down to unlock her door, Myla put a hand on his arm, her eyes full of gratitude. "I owe you so much."

Nick wanted much more than just gratitude, but he couldn't tell her that. "Stop worrying," he said in a reassuring tone. "Now, let's go take care of Jesse."

Chapter Eight

"It's not your fault," Nick said softly as he handed Myla the cup of icy soda. All around them, hospital personnel whizzed by, taking care of the business of healing the sick.

Myla looked around, a concerned expression darkening her face. "I've been so busy lately. I should have seen this coming. I've always been able to gauge her allergies before, but I just thought she'd caught another cold."

"You had no way of knowing it would turn into pneumonia," he told her as he urged her to sit down on the mauve floral couch in the pediatric waiting room of Schumpert Medical Center. "This stuff is very tricky."

"But I should have been more careful," Myla said, holding her head against one hand. "She's been so sick all winter, and I just kept pumping her full of medicine and sending her to school. I can't believe I didn't catch this in time."

Nick put an arm around her, then squeezed her shoulder for reassurance. "You've had a lot on your mind."

A burly, gray-haired doctor came marching up the hall from the pediatric ward. Spotting Myla and Nick, he halted in front of them. "Ms. Howell, I'm Dr. Redmond." After giving Myla a brisk handshake, he spoke to her in a hushed tone. "You've got one very sick little girl on your hands. We'll need to keep her a few days. She's very congested."

Myla put down her cup of soda with shaky hands. "Will she be all right?"

"I think we can help her," the doctor said. "We've already started administering antibiotics, but it's hard to pinpoint whether this was brought on by a bacterial infection or her allergies. We'll run tests to be sure. We've got her under oxygen until she can breath a little better on her own."

"Whatever it takes, Dr. Redmond," Nick said, his arm around Myla's waist. "I'll cover all the costs."

"Of course, Mr. Rudolph. Anything for the son of Joseph and Ruth Rudolph. Your mother was a special woman. We all miss her very much."

"Me, too," Nick replied. Then, "Just take care of Jesse for me, okay?"

"That we can do." Giving Myla another pat

of assurance, the doctor said, "You can see her now, Ms. Howell."

After the doctor told them he'd check back with them later, Myla looked up at Nick. She was already feeling tremendous guilt because of Jesse's illness. Now, she had the added burden of owing Nick yet again. Maybe if she hadn't been so distracted these past few weeks, if she'd kept her mind on her children's welfare instead of obsessing about Nick, this wouldn't have happened.

Her tone firm, she said, "I can't let you pay for this. I'll use the money I've been saving."

"Myla…" Nick pulled her out of the hallway, away from prying eyes and ears. "Don't think about all of that right now. Your little girl is sick and you don't have insurance. I can help you."

In spite of his good intentions, Myla felt ashamed for having to rely on him, and even more ashamed that she'd let Jesse get so sick. "And what about the next time, and the time after that? Nick, don't you see, you're stepping in to take care of me." Her voice cracking, she added, "Which means, I can't even take care of my daughter on my own!"

The frustration in her eyes only made Nick want to protect her even more. She blamed herself for this, no doubt. And, she probably wanted to blame him, too. "Listen," he said in a gentle tone, "this isn't your fault. And I don't mind whatever comes our way. I want to take care of you."

"I've got to learn to handle things on my own," she retorted, a desperation in her words. "I've got to be more careful from now on." Giving him an imploring look, she grabbed his arm. "Nick, she's so sick."

Nick pulled her close in spite of her resistance. "All the more reason to let me help—this time. Stop worrying about being so self-reliant and concentrate on your daughter." Pushing her hair away from her temple, he looked down at her. "And would you please stop apologizing and thanking me for my generosity. I'm not a saint or a martyr, Myla, but I refuse to let you do this on your own. End of discussion."

"Why?" she had to ask, the humiliation of being needy fighting with her love for him. "Why do you insist on being my knight in shining armor?"

Hearing her ask that question, Nick wondered why himself. Maybe because he *needed* to do something. He couldn't stand by any longer and watch her struggle. Not because she was a widow with two children; not because she didn't have a decent place to live or a good job; but because... he was in love with her. The urge to tell her so hit him with the force of the wind whipping outside the hospital windows. He stared at her, wanted to tell her, but her look of dread and defeat stopped him. "Because you need me," he said.

Myla couldn't deny that. Just having him here made this easier. Sonny had always insisted Jesse didn't have allergies and that Myla was just babying the little girl. Nick hadn't even questioned it. Yes, she needed him. But she wasn't willing to admit just how much. Not yet.

"I'll pay you back, a little each week," she declared, her tone stubborn.

He reached for her, gently urging her back into his arms. "Okay. We'll work out the details later."

"I want to see my daughter now," she whispered. Then, "Nick, I am really grateful to you. Thanks, again."

Gratitude. Nick had never had much time for that kind of mushy sentiment. Now, as he stood staring out the window of Jesse's room, he thought how ironic it was that he'd fallen in love with a woman who thanked him almost daily for his generosity. He'd dated lots of women and they'd all had some sort of pedigree attached: old money, new money, star quality, socialite connections, snobbish attitudes, but never had one of them given him any gratitude.

Myla was different. Stubborn. Determined. Firm in her beliefs. And bound to show the world she could handle things on her own. Would she resent him for always rushing to her rescue?

Jesse stirred under the oxygen tent, bringing Myla up out of her chair and Nick back from the window.

"Mama?" A small hand reached out in the darkened room, and Myla was immediately there to take it.

"I'm right here, honey. It's all right. Try to go back to sleep."

She patted Jesse's hand, her eyes meeting Nick's over the bed. He seemed so distant, so far away in his thoughts as he stood there by the window, watching the sun set. Now he moved to stare down at her daughter, concern evident in his dark eyes.

"She's drifted off again," he whispered. "Want to step out and get some fresh air?"

"Maybe in a minute." She walked around the bed to join him. "She looks so tiny and helpless, lying there like that. I'm afraid to leave her."

He wrapped an arm around her waist to tug her close. "Then we'll stay."

Myla leaned against him, glad for the support. "It's so late. Why don't you go back home? You've been at one hospital with Henny, and now this with Jesse. You need to go home and get some rest."

"I don't mind. I don't want to leave you."

Touched, she asked, "Does being here make you think about your mother?"

"Yes, but it's better now." He kissed the top of her head, then said, "You know, after Mother died, my father donated a huge sum of money to help build a new cancer wing. But he never set foot in this hospital again, and neither did I, until today."

Myla lifted her head to gaze into his eyes, her heart going out to him. "Nick, why didn't you say something? You didn't have to stay."

"Yes, I did. You were right, Myla. I can't blame the doctors or God for my mother's illness. I know miracles happen everyday, but sometimes there's just no way to save someone you love. When I think of all the time I wasted, blaming others, wallowing in my misery, I wonder sometimes how I got through each day. Now, after having been around you, I'm finding it easier to accept. Why was it so hard before?"

She held her arms on his shoulders, smiling up at him. "Maybe because your grief was getting in the way. You weren't open or willing to listen then. Now, you are."

He threw his head back, lifting his eyes to the sky. "It sure takes a heavy load off my back."

"That's the beauty of having someone higher to turn to. We don't have to waste our energy worrying about things we can't change."

"But we can concentrate on the things we can change."

"Exactly."

"Well, then, Ms. Howell, take some of your own advice, and stop worrying about your daughter. I predict she's going to be just fine."

Myla shot Jesse a loving look. "I certainly hope so."

"Would you feel better if we said a little prayer?"

"I've been praying," she admitted, "but, yes, I'd appreciate it if you'd pray along with me."

He did, asking for Jesse's quick recovery and asking for the courage to go out and help others who might be worse off. Because, it would take courage and strength to make a visible change within himself. But he intended to do it.

Jesse's harsh cough broke into his thoughts. Myla wasted little time slipping out of his embrace to rush to her daughter's side. Nick watched helplessly as Myla soothed the little girl with a few gentle words.

The tender scene shattered his heart into a million pieces, reminding him of how his father had held his mother, trying in vain to ease her horrible pain. Had his father been weak then, or had he simply been overcome by love and grief? Maybe his love for Ruthie had been his strength.

Bitterly, Nick wondered if he'd misjudged his father, after all. Was it possible to be vulnerable and still remain strong?

If this was a test, he was certainly going to try to live up to it. Walking to the bed, he leaned over Jesse. "We're both right here, honey. Do you need anything?"

The little girl reached out her hand, taking Nick's stronger one. He wrapped his fingers around her frail little bones, his heart bursting with such a protective warmth that he wondered how anyone ever managed to get through fatherhood at all.

"I'm scared," she whispered, her big blue-green eyes wide and misty.

Nick gripped the tiny fingers clinging to his hand. "We all get scared sometimes, Jesse. But you're going to be all right. I won't let anything bad happen to you."

Myla looked at the man holding her daughter's hand, her own tears mirroring the moisture she saw gathering in the depths of his eyes. He didn't know it, but he'd just given her the one thing all his money couldn't buy. He'd given her that part of himself he'd been hiding from the world. By admitting his own fears, Nick Rudolph had shown just exactly how much courage he had.

And, he'd given her the ability to trust again.

* * *

Later, when dawn colored the trees outside a vivid newborn pink, Myla roused Nick out of his cramped position on a nearby chair. "I'm worried about Patrick. Will you go and check on Lydia and him before he goes to school? And get some rest while you're there."

Half asleep, Nick smiled at her bossy nature, feeling warm and content with the new intimacy that had developed between them during these past few hours. "How's the patient?"

"She's breathing better."

He got up to stretch long and hard. "Ah, we made it through the night."

Myla's warm gaze touched on his face. "Yes, we did."

He shook the creaks out of his neck. "Okay, then, I'll check on our other wards, then I guess I'll see you for lunch, maybe." With that, he headed for the darkened door.

Myla handed him his coat. "Nick?"

He turned, an expectant look on his face.

"Give Patrick a kiss for me."

With that, he took the two steps to reach her. "I'll do better than that. I'll take him one from his mother."

Surprised, Myla lifted on tiptoe as he kissed her solidly on the lips. When he reluctantly let her go, she managed to say, "Well, thank you, I think."

Nick's wide grin cut through the darkened room. "Now that's the kind of thanks I can live with."

"She's much better."

Myla held her daughter's hand, rubbing her fingers back and forth over the soft skin as she waited for Dr. Redmond to give them an update. Nick sat nearby, his relief evident as he smiled over at Jesse.

After three days in the hospital, the little girl was getting restless. "Can I go home? I miss Shredder."

Dr. Redmond held his hands together, absently pivoting on his tennis shoes, his eyes fixed on Jesse. "The antibiotics have kicked in," he said, his gray brows knotted together. "She showed all the signs of having bacterial pneumonia, but based on her history with allergies…I'd say this was more an allergic reaction than a case of pneumonia. This dry heat we use to stay warm, coupled with her not being able to get out in the fresh air, probably triggered all of this. But we still need to pinpoint exactly what caused her to have such an adverse reaction."

"What should we do?" Nick asked, his own

gaze centered on Jesse. "What do you think caused this?"

"Oh, could be several things." The doctor eased over to Jesse, his smile reassuring. "I'm sure regular old dust and mold contributed a lot to it. Pine straw, dry leaves, and as I said, dry heat—a humidifier would help there."

"She does have a hard time with mold," Myla said. "I always kept our house as clean as possible to avoid provoking her allergies."

"Yeah," Jesse added hoarsely. "Mama wouldn't let me play in the barn back home." Then giving Myla a sheepish look, she added, "But I did help Lydia rake pine straw the other day. Me and Patrick and Shredder played in it."

Myla shot her daughter a reprimanding look, then quickly amended her feelings to reprimand herself instead. "I'm sorry, honey. I should have told Lydia, but I never thought about all those pine trees in the backyard."

"Hey," Nick interjected, "it's okay. Now that we know, we'll all be more careful. And we'll go out and buy a humidifier right now."

The doctor flexed his shoulders, then smiled down at Jesse. "Who's this Shredder I keep hearing about?"

"My cat," Jesse piped up, beaming.

The doctor stopped smiling. "You have a cat?"

Myla nodded. "Yes, a stray. We kind of

adopted him." Seeing the doctor's disapproving look, she asked, "Do you think she's allergic to the cat?"

Carefully wording his statement so as not to upset Jesse, the doctor told them, "No one can predict these things. She picked up a bug and her allergies collided with it. It's that simple. We'll send her home with some medicine for the symptoms, but I'd like to do a new set of allergy tests and start her on shots once we find the culprits. But even then, you'll need to keep her away from dust, and that tempting pine straw." Pulling Myla aside, he whispered, "And I'd advise getting rid of the cat."

Later, as they zoomed away from the hospital to take Jesse home, Nick turned to Myla. "What if she's allergic to Shredder? We'll have to give him to someone else."

"She'll be devastated," Myla whispered, glancing over her shoulder to make sure Jesse wasn't listening. "But if it's dangerous to her health, we won't have a choice."

"Of course, I can keep the cat after you move out," he offered, thinking the tiny animal would help ease his own loneliness. "Maybe by the time you get a new place, we'll know one way or the other."

"That would make Jesse feel better, I'm sure." Giving him a meaningful look, she added, "Now

I'm worried about moving at all. If we do go to Magnolia House…well, it's very old and not in the best of condition. I hope the move won't provoke another allergy attack."

"That is something to consider," he said, feeling a wave of hope rise in his heart. "And wouldn't it be a shame now, if you just had to go on living at my big, old house?"

Myla stared ahead, acutely aware of how Nick had talked to the doctor as if Jesse were his own child. But the reality of this was that Jesse was her responsibility. "I can't do that, Nick. And you know why."

He maneuvered the car through a busy intersection, then gave her his full attention. "Why? You'd still be my employee and we have plenty of chaperons."

"It's not that. You've been very understanding about our relationship."

"Yes, I've learned extreme patience. You know you can count on that. So, what's the problem?"

"It's just not right, Nick. I need to get my own place for my own peace of mind, as well as your standing in the community."

Taking one hand away from the steering wheel, he gave her a sharp look. "My standing? What are you talking about?"

Gritting her teeth, she plunged right in. "Carolyn could make trouble for us. She hinted at it the other day. She said people would talk if they knew we were…living together, so to speak, especially if they found out we had feelings for each other. I can't put you through that, and I certainly won't expose my children to that kind of ridicule."

Stopping for a red light, Nick banged the wheel of the car. "Well, you're right about one thing. I do need to pay Carolyn a little visit. And when I'm finished, I think she'll be straight on a lot of things."

"Don't…don't say anything you'll regret," she cautioned. "I don't want Carolyn to think I'm telling you things about her that aren't true."

"I know what to say," he assured her. "You taught me patience. And I'll sure need it with Carolyn."

True to his word, Nick did have a long talk with Carolyn Parker. But to Myla's dismay, instead of making it clear that he was ending things with Carolyn, Nick invited the blonde to serve on the grassroots committee he was forming to help the homeless.

"If she sees that I've changed for the better and that I still care for her as a good friend, maybe she'll leave us alone," he explained to Myla. "Besides, we've done nothing wrong, so we have nothing to hide."

Myla wasn't so sure, but she did agree that they had nothing to be ashamed of. She was working for Nick, nothing more. No matter that she loved him dearly. She'd do the right thing, for her children's sake.

Tonight, she stood in the kitchen preparing a hearty dinner for the ad hoc committee Nick was heading up. The team included Nick and Lydia, a reporter from one of the television stations to bring in publicity, Carolyn because of her connections within the society of Shreveport, and Grant—because Lydia had insisted he was sensitive to the needs of the homeless.

Now, Carolyn came into the kitchen, her cool gaze slipping over Myla to settle on the pot of gumbo Myla had stewing on the stove.

"Have you heard the news?" Carolyn asked, flipping on the nearby television set. "I thought you'd like to know."

"Know what?" Myla asked warily.

To her surprise, the reporter who was due here any minute was on the early news, covering a story on Magnolia House. The sound of hammering echoed behind the smiling dark-haired newswoman as she explained how a group of local companies had banded together to donate a new heating and cooling unit to the transitional shelter.

"These men are installing the new unit while

we have this mild break in the winter weather. And they're cleaning and renovating the ancient air ducts, too," the reporter, a lady named Brooke Alexander, explained.

"A new unit?" Myla's eyes widened. Thinking about the mold and dust that would be cleared away, she remembered Dr. Redmond's warning. That wouldn't be a problem for Jesse now.

"This gesture of kindness is costing a small fortune," the reporter continued, "but these companies banded together to pay all the expenses."

Suspicious, Myla leaned over the counter. A thought popped into her head, but she couldn't quite put it to words. Anxious to hear more, she turned up the volume.

"The leader of this project has asked to remain anonymous," Ms. Alexander said, "but sources tell us he runs one of the most successful oil companies in Louisiana."

No doubt who that was, Myla mused, her gaze locking with Carolyn's. "Nick did this, didn't he?"

Carolyn nodded slowly, no hostility in her eyes. "Yes, I believe he did. He'd mentioned it to me when he asked me to serve on this committee, and I guess he couldn't wait to get started on things. You must be very proud of him."

"I am," Myla admitted. "And you should be, too."

Carolyn came around the counter to sample the gumbo. Taking a spoon, she dipped a helping, then held it away to cool for a minute. "I am. And Myla, I want to apologize for the way I acted the other day. I've always been a sore loser."

Myla searched Carolyn's face, then, seeing the sincerity in the other woman's eyes, went back to her task of slicing French bread. "You're not a loser, Carolyn. You're a lovely woman and I know Nick cares about you. I'm just sorry if I've caused you any heartache."

"You didn't. Nick did. But I'm over it now. You see, I've never seen Nick like this. He really has changed. And when he took the time to come and really talk to me, in a way we haven't talked in years…well, I knew I'd never win him back. All he could talk about was you and how he was going to form this corporation to help the homeless."

Myla chuckled softly. "He's pretty determined, once he sets his mind to something."

Carolyn grabbed a slice of bread and dipped it into the gumbo for one more taste. "Yes, and you'd better remember that."

"Oh, I'm well aware of it," Myla answered. "But thanks for the warning."

Carolyn lifted one brow. "You know, I thought Nick was married to his work. Maybe I was wrong. Maybe I just wasn't the right person to pry him away from Rudolph Oil. I think you might succeed, though."

"If anything happens," Myla said, stressing the *if,* "we will have to take it slow. I have to be very sure."

"Just don't hurt him," Carolyn warned. "That would devastate him at this point."

Myla watched as Carolyn pranced out of the room. Maybe she should consider her feelings for Nick long and hard. After all, she'd spouted platitudes to him, talked to him, helped him to find his faith again. If she let him down, he might lose all the trust he'd gained over the last few weeks, and never regain it again.

Had Carolyn really been trying to understand, or was this warning just another way for her to fuel Myla's own doubts?

"Trust in God," Myla said as she absently stirred the thick gumbo. "And put a little trust in Nick, too."

Now, if she could just learn to trust herself.

Chapter Nine

After Myla served coffee and dessert, everyone gathered around the empty dining table with pads and pens. Nick stole away and found her in the kitchen, busy loading the dishwasher. Stopping in the arched doorway, he remembered watching her like this before. How natural she looked, so domestic and womanly, so beautiful. She was the type of woman who loved having a home to call her own.

Yet she didn't have any place to call her own.

"Need some help there?" he called, lifting his shoulder off the doorway to push toward her.

Myla pivoted at the sound of his voice. Noting how attractive he looked in his old jeans and faded red polo shirt, she calmed her tap-dancing nerves to a slow waltz. "How's the planning committee going?"

"For the moment, it's going without me."

Handing her a glass, he added, "We were hoping you'd join us."

She shook her head. "I...I used to serve on committees, too many of them. Sonny resented it, but he couldn't tell me to stop—all part of his carefully constructed public image. I've already told Lydia I'll be glad to work behind the scenes, but I don't want to be on the committee. It's nice to just do my job now."

She didn't tell him that since Jesse's illness, she'd made a firm commitment to sticking strictly to business—just until she could get out on her own and get a proper perspective on her feelings for Nick.

Nick didn't let her get away so easily. "But isn't this part of your job? I mean, aren't you the one who told me we had to do something, make some changes?"

She lifted her brows, stopping her busywork to stare up at him. "I intend to do something. I'll stamp and fold mail-outs. I'll make copies and run errands. I'll even cook for the volunteers."

"And stay hidden away, just like you once accused me of doing?"

"That sounds like a challenge."

"It is a challenge. None of us know what we're doing in there. But you, you've been there. You could be a big help, and I want you...because you have firsthand experience."

Placing one hand on her hip, she teased him to hide the warm feelings his words provoked. "Oh, and since you're the boss, I guess that's an order?"

He smiled when he saw the twinkle in her eyes. "Yes, I guess it is. But I'm asking, not demanding. And I'm not asking to enhance my public image, but because I care."

"You have changed."

"Okay, okay. I get the point. Are you going to help us or not?"

She turned on the dishwasher, then took one more look around the spotless kitchen. "Okay. Guess it wouldn't hurt to just sit in and listen. Let me check on the children, and then I'll be right in."

He waited for her, watching as she kissed her sleeping children, his heart helplessly opening another fraction because of the sweetness of her nurturing strength. Then when Jesse opened her eyes and called out to her mother, he stopped at the door.

"Mama, where's Shredder? I want him to sleep with me."

Myla leaned over her daughter, placing a hand on Jesse's face. "You know Shredder is off-limits in here until we're sure you're completely well, honey. He's just fine in his little bed out in the garage, and during the day he gets to roam around the rest of the house."

Jesse looked so sad, Nick couldn't help it. He stepped back into the room. "Your mother's right, sweetie. You might be allergic to that crazy cat."

Jesse sat up, her big eyes imploring Nick. "But I love Shredder. You aren't going to make us get rid of him, are you, Mr. Nick?"

Nick squatted by the bed, so he could see Jesse better. "Of course not. He just has to stay out of Henny's rooms for a while, until we're sure you're not allergic."

That seemed to calm the little girl. "Okay. That's all I was worried about. Mr. Nick, please take care of Shredder for me—after we move into the shelter."

Nick glanced up at Myla, then looked back down at Jesse. Swallowing the tightness in his throat, he said, "I will. Shredder will always have a home here."

"Even if I can't come to visit?"

"Even if you can't come to visit."

Jesse lay back down then, her voice so soft, Nick had to strain to hear her words. "'Cause Shredder was just like us, wasn't he? He didn't have any other place to go."

Myla sat down on the bed then to gather her daughter close. Her words were husky, but Nick heard the tremor in her voice. "That's right, honey. Mr. Nick took us in when we didn't have a place to stay, and I know he'll take care of Shredder for us. You don't have to worry about that."

"I promise," Nick said, his eyes on the woman holding the little girl. "Always."

Myla tucked Jessica back in, then pulled the door partly closed before turning to Nick. "Nick, I—"

"Don't say thank you, please," he whispered. "You don't owe me anything. Can't you see, you and your children have redeemed me. I was so lonely, so alone, so bitter. Now, I have something to fight for. And I will fight for you, Myla. Oh, I know you're holding off on any decisions and I know you have to do things your way, such as writing me those checks for the doctor's bill. But I won't give up. I don't give up too easily."

"I have noticed that about you," she said, stopping him in the alcove just outside the door to the dining room. "Nick, I'm really proud of what you did for Magnolia House."

Shrugging, he said, "I don't know what you're talking about."

"Yes, you do. You went in there and overhauled their heating and cooling system. It was a very unselfish thing to do."

He lowered his head, not used to being heralded for doing good deeds. "I did it for Jesse."

"I know that," she said softly, "and you helped all those other people in the process."

"That's me, just an all-around good guy."

"You are a good guy. Jesse obviously thinks you hung the moon."

He shook his head, then grinned. "No, I just hired someone to do it for me." Then turning serious, he said, "Your daughter and I have grown closer in our efforts to keep Shredder from being booted out of the house."

Myla had noticed that bond between her daughter and this man, especially tonight. It would be so hard to pull her children out of the safe environment Nick had provided for them. "It was very sweet of you to talk to her about Shredder."

"I talked to her because I care about her—and that wild cat. And like I said, I don't give up easily. Not even on a woman who thinks she has to do everything her way."

No, he wasn't one to give up, Myla thought. She had to make him see her fears, though. Make him understand that this wasn't so simple. "But *I* don't have anything to offer you, Nick. I'm so afraid I'll make the same mistake twice."

He held her, his hands firm on her arms. "Look at me, Myla. I'm not like Sonny. I'd never treat you the way he did. I'd never hurt you."

"I want to believe that," she said, hoping to

make him understand. "I do. And really, it's not you I'm worried about. It's me. I don't want to let you down."

Amazed at her self-doubt, Nick said, "You haven't let me down so far. You don't give yourself enough credit, Myla."

Voicing her worst fears, she said, "But what if Carolyn is right? What if you're just intrigued with me because I'm your new cause? What if these feelings aren't strong enough to carry us through in the long run?"

He hissed a bitter laugh. "Do you think I feel sorry for you? Is that it? Do you think I'm doing all of this out of pity?"

She dropped her head. "Maybe. I don't know."

He gently tugged her close, then wrapped his arms around her waist. "Myla, Myla, sometimes I *envy* you. I envy your strength and your courage and your convictions. I've wanted to help you all along, but…I don't feel sorry for you. You don't allow that."

She lifted her head, her eyes searching his. "You've changed so much since that first night. I just have to be sure, Nick. Very sure."

He touched a hand to her hair. "Well, I am sure. I was lost the night I saw you standing in the middle of that road." Seeing the stubborn glint in her eyes, he plunged on. "I'd always heard Lydia talking about Magnolia House, but

I never had the time or the inclination to go to the place myself. Well, the other day, after what the doctor told us about Jesse's condition, I did go. I had to check the place out before I could bring myself to let you move in there."

He stopped, taking a long breath, his eyes going dark. "When I saw the other children—the ones I don't even know, living in those cramped apartments, wearing clothes donated by other people and eating food provided by someone else—I understood why Lydia does the things she does, and why you gave that old man your plasma money.

"It broke my heart to see those families, but they all had one thing in common. They were all fighting this thing together, and they seemed secure and happy. And I kept remembering that Bible verse from Proverbs about those who are rich yet have nothing, and those who are poor, yet have great riches."

"I know the verse," Myla said, thinking of how many times she'd counted her blessings, even when she had nothing worldly in her possession. "It's hard to grasp, though, when you see homeless people on the street."

He nodded. "Yes, especially when you live in a mansion and have a fat bank account, yet still manage to gripe your way through each day. I'm ashamed to think I never really cared about what was going on around me before."

She patted him on the arm. "Well, now you do care. And that's what's so important." If nothing else, she and Nick would have that bond to share. And she'd be remiss to turn him down now, when *he* was asking for her help. Smiling up at him, she said, "I'll serve on your committee, Nick. I'll do whatever I can."

He gave her a quick, reassuring kiss, then took her into the long dining room. Lifting a hand to the others at the table, he announced, "We have a new recruit. Myla has agreed to serve with us— and not just behind the scenes."

Lydia clapped, her smile broad. "Oh, good. We've got the preliminary plans for the charity ball laid out and we've registered our incorporation papers with the state—we're calling our organization Hope, Faith and Love, Incorporated. But Myla, we need to ask you something."

Eyeing her warily, Myla said, "Sure, I think."

Brooke Alexander, the reporter who'd joined up to promote her television station's charitable image, said, "We've come into some property, a house in the old Highland District, and we're going to recruit people to remodel it for a deserving family. From everything Lydia and Nick have told us tonight, you're eligible to apply for it."

Her interest growing, Myla sat down. "I've

been trying to find out more about how to qualify for one of those low-cost houses. Are you saying I could possibly get this house?"

"We think so," Grant said, tapping his ink pen on his notepad. "The house has already been donated, free and clear. All you need to do is fill out the application and wait for the board's approval. But, whether you get the house or not, we'd like you to give a speech at the charity ball—telling about your situation."

Lydia gave Grant a look of total adoration. Nick, however, didn't have time tonight to fume at his little sister's obvious infatuation. He was too busy studying Myla's reaction to the news of the house. Would she be pleased?

Too astonished to notice anything else, Myla asked, "How many people will be at this event?"

Lydia leaned forward. "If all goes as planned, about two to three hundred."

"Three hundred people!" Myla shook her head. "I couldn't possibly."

Carolyn gave her a level stare. "Nick thinks you have a story to tell."

"He would." Myla sighed, then ran a shaking hand through her long tresses. Could she really face all those people with her humiliating story? "I'll…I'll have to think about this."

Lydia jotted down some more notes. "Well, we don't have much time. We've already formed a solid board of directors, and we're setting up the bylaws now. We're shooting for mid-April for the membership kickoff, with the ball as our first fund-raiser."

Myla shook her head. "That's only a couple of months. No, I can't. I'm not ready to talk about everything that's happened to me."

Nick spoke softly from the doorway behind her. "Think of all the people you'll be helping."

His dark eyes washed her with a warmth that left her mystified. This new Nick was even more intriguing than the old reserved one. And rather than making her into a charity case, he was working toward helping her in a positive way. He was willing to let her make it on her own, without any pressure about their relationship. This would be a risk, but it would also give her the freedom to make her own choices. And she'd have a home again.

"Hope, Faith and Love," she said, her eyes meeting Nick's. "These three."

"And the greatest of these is love," he reminded her gently.

Biting her bottom lip, she nodded slowly. "I'll be so nervous, and we don't even know if I'll get the house."

"You'll win the house and every heart at the

ball," Nick said. And he'd see to it personally, if it would make her regain her self-confidence.

"Looks like she's already won one," Brooke teased, her keen eyes lighting on Nick. "Maybe that's the real story."

"Yeah," Carolyn added, getting up to leave. "And if you can win ruthless Nick Rudolph over, you don't need to worry about anyone else in this town."

Myla didn't miss the sarcasm or the hint of regret in the other woman's parting words. And apparently from the interested look in her eyes, neither did Brooke Alexander.

"I don't want to make a big deal out of this," Nick warned the reporter. "Let's keep my involvement low-key, okay?"

"Sure, Nick." The woman's smile was practiced and precise. "Just the facts, I promise."

Myla waited until the others had left, then turned to Nick. "Did you plan this—getting me involved, I mean—just to shift the spotlight from yourself?"

He gave her a level look. "No. Actually it was Carolyn's idea to have you speak at the fundraiser. You've managed to win her over, too. Quite a coup."

Myla looked skeptical. "Well, if I get my own

place, I'll be away from you. Probably why she suggested this."

"Whoa, I hadn't thought about it that way. Carolyn's pretty crafty, but I do believe she's sincere about this. She didn't flirt with me once tonight. In fact, I think she's found a new catch—my friend from the city council. He's single and up-and-coming, just her type, and Lydia had the good sense to seat them next to each other at some stuffy social event the other night."

Myla laughed in spite of her worries, then said, "I appreciate your board's considering me for the house, and of course I understand I might not qualify. I just hope you didn't bully anybody into doing this—"

He shook his head. "I'm doing what I thought you wanted most in the world—I'm helping you to find a place to live."

Realizing he was right, she didn't argue with him any further. This had been her goal, her dream all along. This was her chance to prove herself. And maybe, this was Nick's chance to prove himself, too.

"I'll be at your fancy ball," she said at last.

He gave her a look that told her everything, yet revealed nothing. Did she see regret in his eyes, or relief, or maybe both?

"You can wear the green dress."

Gripping her hands together, Myla looked away, sweet memories of that special Christmas night coloring her mind. "Yes, that is the only elegant thing I own."

"Wear it for me," he whispered, reaching out to draw her into his arms. "And we'll come home and have a turkey sandwich and pound cake, and we'll dance underneath the stars."

"Sounds perfect," she said as she leaned into his kiss.

Except by that time, she might be living in a different home.

"I'm getting a house," Myla told Grant a few weeks later as they cleaned up after the breakfast rush at the coffeehouse.

"That's great, isn't it?" he asked, giving her a questioning look. "I mean, this is all you've talked about since you started working here. Now you won't have to live in the homeless shelter, right?"

"Right." Myla finished making a fresh pot of French vanilla decaf. "At least I can bypass that part of the transition. I wasn't looking forward to shifting my children around."

Grant stopped stacking dishes to stare over at her. "So, things are working out for you. Then why do you look like you've just lost your best friend?"

Myla started doodling on an order pad lying by the cash register. Grant was very astute and sensitive. And right on target about her mood today. She had been down since learning that the board of directors for Hope, Faith and Love had voted for her to be the recipient of their first house.

She didn't know why she was reacting this way, but something just didn't feel right about this. Maybe it had all been too easy, and she surely wasn't used to getting things the easy way. Or maybe, the truth be told, she didn't really want to leave Nick, after all.

Deciding she could trust Grant, she said, "Oh, who am I kidding? It's because I love working for Nick, and I love cleaning that big old house of his, and cooking and pretending I'm a house-wife again."

Grant nodded, his poetic eyes gazing over at her with a too knowing expression. "Oh, I see. You've found a home and you don't want to leave it, because you have feelings for the owner. Does he know how you feel?"

Embarrassed, Myla placed a bundle of clean forks in a nearby holder. "*I* don't know how I feel. On the one hand, I think I love Nick and could be completely happy with him. But on the other hand, I still don't know how he really feels about me. And I have to be sure, not only of him, but of myself. So, I figure the only way I can do that is to go ahead and move out on my own and see if we can hold on to what we think we have."

Grant rolled his eyes. "This is complicated, huh?"

"Very." Turning to a customer, Myla handed him his espresso, then took his dollar. "And I don't want to burden you with the details."

"Hey, that's what friends are for," Grant said, his gentle blue eyes touching hers. "You'll find your way, Myla. After all, you've come this far."

"Yes, I have," she reminded herself. "And I am excited about the house. It's so cute. It needs work, of course, and I'm required to put in five hundred hours of sweat equity to help fix it up, but I can't wait. I get a twenty-year, interest-free loan, so it's really going to be mine."

"That sounds fair," Grant remarked, straining as he reached for some clean coffee cups. "Need any help?"

"Yes. We rely on volunteers to help do most of the work. Nick has set this corporation up so that everything is donated, including time."

"I'll be there," Grant said, pushing his glasses up on his long nose. "Especially if it means I'll get to see Lydia more."

Smiling at last, Myla nudged him with her elbow. "How's that relationship going, Romeo?"

Grant sighed, then shook his head. "Let's just say, I know what you mean about Nick Rudolph. That man's hard to get to know." He waved his hands. "One minute he's teasing me, the next, he's glaring at me."

Myla could picture Nick doing exactly that; he'd certainly shifted moods on her enough. "So, in other words, things could be great between you and Lydia if Nick would just back off?"

"Something like that," Grant replied. "Her big brother thinks I have less than honorable intentions toward Lydia, but I really like her, you know."

"I do know," Myla said as she took the money for a customer's cookie and coffee. "Lydia has a kind heart and she's very serious about helping other people."

"She sure is," Grant agreed readily. "I'll admit I didn't believe that at first. I thought she was just some bored rich kid out to appease her sense of social duty. But now that I've spent some time with her, I can tell she's really sincere. Did you know she's thinking of going back to college to become a bona fide counselor? She wants to do more than just volunteer a few hours a week."

Surprised, Myla gave him a wide-eyed look. "Does Nick know that? No, of course, he couldn't, or I'm sure I would have heard all about it."

"No, not yet," Grant said, his voice low and worried. "She's been trying to figure out a way to spring the news on him."

"That should be interesting." Then, wanting to reassure her friend, she said, "Nick means well, Grant. It's just…he's been both Lydia's brother and surrogate parent for so long, he's forgotten how to let go. I think he's turned all his pain into some sort of overprotective focus on his sister."

"Yeah, I know," Grant replied. "And Lydia sure sees it. That's why she's afraid to tell him about her plans. She doesn't want him to lash out at me, or think I put her up to this—which he'll do, I guarantee."

"Maybe I can talk to him," Myla offered. "Smooth the way once Lydia breaks the news?"

"You've got enough to deal with."

"I can handle Nick," Myla said, although she dreaded the tirade once Nick found out about Lydia's plans. "Let me take care of him, and you concentrate on Lydia, okay?"

"Okay," Grant said, "but I can fight my own battles. I'm not afraid of Nick Rudolph."

"Very noble," Myla teased, "but…Nick's really an old softy underneath all that bluster. We both need to remember that."

Grant nodded, then patted Myla on the shoulder. "Well, now that we've discussed both our personal lives, how about we discuss something else that's been on my mind?"

"What's that?" Myla asked, confused by the intense look on his face.

"Adding more to the menu," Grant said. Waving his hand again, he added, "After all, we've made a good team so far."

Relieved, Myla grabbed the computer printout of their profits and losses. "Oh, that reminds me—"

Grant wiped his hands on his white apron, a frown marring his boyish face. "You're not going to quit on me, are you?"

"No, nothing like that." She tapped the ledger with her finger. "I got a call about a catering job—they'd like us to cater a sit-down dinner for about twenty-five people and I'm anxious to test the waters." Before he could answer, she continued, "It's going to be hectic, but I think this is a good opportunity. We'd get lots of publicity."

Grant's eyes lit up. "Are you serious?"

She gave him a playful punch on the arm. "Well, as you just pointed out, we've made great progress so far and this would give us exactly what we'd hoped for, even though it is earlier than we'd planned. We can start building a strong base for our catering company. That is—if you think we're ready?"

Rubbing a hand across his swarthy chin, Grant thought about it for about a minute. "You do have a point, and from the smell of that garlic bread baking, I'd be crazy to let our first catering customers get away without sampling it. After our first hundred thousand or so, we can branch out." Grinning, he extended his hand. "I think it's a good idea. Tell them we accept."

"What's a good idea?"

Myla looked up to find Nick staring across the counter at her, with Lydia right beside him, smiling shyly at Grant. Grant glanced over at Myla, panic in his eyes.

Lydia hopped up on a bar stool, spinning around before she stopped, breathless and giggling. "Hi, Grant."

Nick sat down in a more dignified manner, his curious look moving from Myla to Grant. "You two look as if you've just committed a felony. What's with the guilty faces?"

Before Myla could answer his question, Lydia spoke to Grant again. "How's it been going?"

"Great. It's good...uh, real good. We were just—" He shot Myla a beseeching look.

"We were just going over the books," Myla interjected to stop Grant from stuttering. "Business is picking up."

"That's wonderful," Lydia said, her eyes on

Grant. "By the way, I really enjoyed that movie the other night."

Grant pushed his bifocals up on his nose. "Me, too. Uh…can I get you a cup of coffee?"

Myla glanced at Nick. He was glaring, his dark eyes flashing such a protective fire for his sister, she was surprised he didn't come across the counter to grab poor Grant by the collar.

To waylay any such action, she said, "We've been making plans to branch out, and start our catering services right here from the coffeehouse."

"Really?" Nick spoke at last, a look of disbelief plastered across his face. "Are you sure you're ready to take on more work?"

Trying not to get too defensive, Myla placed a hand on her hip. "With Grant's help, yes, and only after Henny's completely well and back home, of course." There, that should reassure him that she wouldn't slack up on her responsibilities to him. "We've been offered a small catering job, and we just now this very minute decided to go for it."

"Sure did. That's what we were doing when you two showed up." Grant handed Lydia her coffee, then managed to ramble on. "Myla's a real treasure. Since she's started working here, we're becoming famous for our cookies and pastries."

Lydia bobbed her blond head. "Yep, Nick and I have put on a few pounds ourselves since Christmas."

"Speak for yourself," Nick said, his expression relaxing as he patted his tummy. "And pass the double chocolate chip cookies and a cup of that New Orleans blend coffee, please."

Lydia grabbed a cookie as Myla held out the basket. "Grant, you've done a wonderful job with this old building. This is fast becoming one of downtown's most popular spots."

Grant lowered his head and smiled, his face flushing red. "Like I told you, I needed a place to read my incredibly bad poetry."

Lydia looked pleased as punch. "A poet *and* a smart businessman. I like that."

Grant blushed, then offered to show Lydia a new display of paintings they'd hung that very morning.

Nick rolled his eyes as his sister practically skipped away with Grant, then said under his breath, "I think my sister's about to make a conquest. She's been stringing him along for weeks now, in spite of my warnings for her to be careful. I don't think I can bear to watch this anymore."

"Well, don't worry," Myla said, hoping to calm his brotherly concern. "Grant is a good man. He goes to church every Sunday and plays his guitar with the choir at times. And his poetry is very spiritual. He wouldn't hurt a fly."

"Great. My sister falls for the Lord Byron of Coffeeshops."

Myla glanced over at Lydia and Grant. They were deep into their own conversation, both with stars in their eyes. Deciding now wasn't the best time to tell Nick about his sister's plans—in fact, it might be best to let Lydia handle that herself— she told him, "She'll be fine." Then, she added, "What brings you two in this early in the day, anyway?"

"Wrapping up plans for the benefit ball," he explained. "Can we still count on you to make that speech?"

Her stomach twisted into a bowknot, but she quickly calmed it down. "I'll be there, but I'll be busy over the next few weeks working on the house. I got a call today, telling me I passed the application process."

He sat perfectly still, his pride shining in his golden brown eyes. "I knew you would. Need help with the renovations?"

She didn't miss his smug expression. Challenging him, she said, "I expect you to be the first in line."

"You can count on it," he replied, his tone casual. "I need to do something to make up for causing you to miss your spot at Magnolia House."

"Yes, but you've already worked hard to make up for that. Setting up this corporation will help so much, Nick. You're going to make a big difference in this community."

"That's a switch," he said, a look of humility on his face. "But you're right. This is different from just writing a check. I've never worked harder."

"And I'll bet you're enjoying every minute of it."

He gave her a wide smile. "That I am."

Lydia's hands clapping together brought both Myla and Nick's heads around. "Grant has agreed to come to our benefit ball. He can sit at our table, since I just talked him into making a sizable contribution to our cause."

"Lucky Grant," Nick teased, his eyes settling on his bubbly sister. "You never stood a chance, you know," he said to Grant.

Grant's laugh was more from nerves than humor. "I can live with that."

Nick turned back to Myla, his expression blank. "Now if I only can."

"You're doing great," Myla said in an encouraging voice, thinking he was as hard to read as the abstract art hanging on the high walls around them.

He feigned a look of innocence. "Far be it from me to interfere with my sister's social life, even though she's accused me of doing just that. I've got enough problems trying to deal with my own."

Just then, a customer called to Myla. She hurried to get the man his bagel and latte, waving to Nick. "I've got work to do."

"So do I," he said, rising up off his stool. "See you at home?"

"Okay." Myla watched him leave, all the while wondering where exactly her own home was supposed to be.

Dear Lord, show me the way. Do I belong with Nick, or should I make this move out on my own? I leave it in Your hands.

Out on the sidewalk, Nick said a similar prayer of his own. He hoped he'd done the right thing this time. He only knew he was letting the woman he loved go in order to win her back fair and square.

The little voice inside his head reminded him that he hadn't been so fair and square.

He told the little voice to be quiet.

Chapter Ten

"Well, it's finished."

Nick stood back to admire the cottage they'd renovated for the first recipient of the Hope, Faith and Love, Incorporated, Housing for the Homeless. "My neck aches," he added as he rubbed the sore muscles at his shoulders.

Myla saw the pride shining in his eyes. That same pride shined within her heart. "It's beautiful, Nick."

He glanced over at her, one paint-dusted hand still on his neck. "And it's yours. All yours."

Weeks had passed—long weeks of hard work and dedicated hours of remodeling the little house. All the volunteers had left after they'd celebrated with pizza and soft drinks. Jesse and Patrick were running around in the backyard, happy to be in their own home. Shredder had opted to live with Nick and Lydia at the mansion, and Jesse hadn't argued. She planned to visit the cat often. Her allergies were all clear now, but Myla was watching her closely with spring coming up.

Now, Myla walked up onto the tiny front porch, admiring the fresh coat of white paint and the blue-colored shutters. "I'm going to plant azaleas," she told him over her shoulder.

"And don't forget the yellow roses."

"Lots of them."

"I'll help you."

She whirled to lean over the new spindle railing. "You have helped me, from the very beginning. I'll never be able to repay you, Nick."

"You already have," he said, coming up to sit on the gray-painted wooden steps. "You gave me something I never dreamed I could find again— my faith."

"I didn't do it," she explained, lowering herself down beside him. "God did."

"He sent you to me."

"He knows how to deal with ruthless executives."

"Yes, He certainly dealt me a curveball. And not just with you—now I've got that Grant fellow to contend with, also."

"How are things with Lydia and Grant?" she asked, careful that she didn't put her nose into their business without being asked.

Nick gave her a knowing glance. "Don't pretend you don't know a thing about them. I know Lydia confides in you almost daily."

Myla tossed her ponytail off her neck. "Okay, yes, I know a little. But I want to know how *you* feel."

He fell back against a square porch column. "Like I'm losing my baby sister…like I'm losing control."

"Or gaining a brother-in-law?"

Nick held up a hand. "Don't! I'm not ready to hear that yet."

"She could do worse," Myla offered, taking his hand in hers. "And I'm proud of you for staying so *in control*. Lydia has to be able to make her own decisions, good or bad."

"Oh, I'm trying hard to stay sane. Especially since she also informed me she's thinking about becoming a social worker. What's gotten into my sister?"

"How long have you known about that?" Myla questioned, surprised that he hadn't ranted and raved about it.

"She told me last night." At Myla's questioning look, he added, "Don't worry. I handled it with brotherly concern and complete calm. You've taught me patience, see? And as you just pointed out, the good Lord has dealt me a whole new set of challenges."

Myla couldn't help but love him all over again. He looked so completely, utterly confused. And so adorable. "But you took what He dealt you and did something positive. And now look."

He lifted his head to look around the peaceful, tree-shaded neighborhood, refusing to feel guilty about her happiness. Spring was just around the corner; already the dogwoods and crape myrtles were starting to bud. He shouldn't feel so lousy—he'd only given the woman he loved the very thing she wanted most in the world.

To hide his overactive conscience, he said, "This is only the beginning. We have two other houses lined up for this summer and fall."

Myla leaned back to take a long breath of the clear, crisp air. "Everything's so beautiful today. So green and fresh. The air smells so rich."

"All is right with the world," Nick said, his tone light in spite of the great sadness coloring his heart. "My sister's changing right before my eyes. Henny's glad to be home, and she's taking things easy. You have a good job with Grant and your catering business. And I've just lost... a wonderful housekeeper."

Myla's heart shifted into an erratic beat. She wanted to thank him for keeping this light, but she didn't think she could voice the words. So instead, she said, "I left you a pound cake in the pantry."

His eyes went all warm and misty. "I'll savor each bite."

Myla sat still, the awkward silence surrounding her. This was it; this was the moment she'd dreamed about since that cold, dark night in her car. She had her own home again, but it was a bittersweet victory.

How could she say goodbye to Nick? She should be happy; she had a place to call her own, at last. Was it wrong to want to be with him?

As if sensing her doubts, Nick looked across at her, his dark eyes holding hers. "I'll miss you so much."

Now, why did he have to go and say that? Swallowing back the tears threatening her eyes, she said, "I know. But we agreed we'd see each other a lot. At church, at the HFL meetings, and you can come over for pizza anytime."

His laugh was stilted. "I'll probably be over a lot. Henny won't be able to cook those elaborate meals anymore. We're both on a low-fat diet now."

"I'll come and help out," she offered, her heart melting. She wanted to run to him and hold him in her arms forever. But…he needed time and so did she. At least, that's what she kept telling herself.

He got up to leave. "I expect you to, but not

tonight. Right now, you need to enjoy your first night in your new house."

"Nick?" she called. "Your parents would be so proud of what you've done."

That statement brought his head around. "Do you really think so?"

"Yes, I do."

He came back to lift one foot up onto the steps, his gaze searching her face. "I want to tell you something—something I haven't told anyone, not even Lydia."

"Okay," she said, patting the place he'd just vacated. "I'm listening."

He sat back down, his hands clasped. "I told you my father died during the oil crisis, but I didn't tell you how he died. He loved my mother so much, but he wasn't much of a church-goer. Mother and Lydia went to church, while Father and I concentrated on the business, always the business. Anyway, when Mother was diagnosed with cancer, well…he literally fell to pieces. And it got much worse after her death.

"I couldn't deal with that—seeing him so weak, so lost. It confused me because he'd always been so strong and firm, so distant and hard to understand. I turned away from him, refusing to help him through the worst time in his life. I couldn't deal with his grief, or mine."

Myla grasped his arm. "Go on. Tell me everything."

"I caused my father's death, Myla."

She gasped, her heart filling with compassion. "What do you mean?"

He continued to look down at the shiny new steps. "We had a terrible argument. He had changed so much, I was only trying to pull him back, to snap him back to reality. I needed him to be strong again. I shouted at him, reminding him of all the things he'd taught me—show no weakness, be a man, don't let anybody get the best of you.

"I think he realized he'd created a monster. I saw the disappointment in his eyes, watched him grip his chest. He died before the paramedics could get there. A massive heart attack. But even after his death, I was still that monster. I became even more cold and uncaring. I didn't have Lydia's strength, or the ability to open my heart."

"Nick, Nick, that's just not true." She brought his head around, pulling him down on her shoulder. "Inside, you were a caring person. You were just still grieving, and no wonder. Your father taught you about business, but he didn't teach you about what's really important in life."

He buried his face in her hair, his words muffled and raw with pain. "I can't do it anymore, Myla. I can't be that person. None of us can go through life without experiencing love. And for such a long time, I was afraid to love because I didn't want to wind up hurt and broken, like my father."

Myla didn't speak. She stroked his hair, understanding he'd carried this burden for so long. He cried softly, draining all the bitterness and the coldness out of his soul, then he lifted his head to look at her.

"I didn't know how to help him. I equated love and need with weakness." Taking her face in his hands, he said, "But you taught me that it's okay to be weak sometimes. You taught me that love is our strength."

"It is, it is," she said, closing her eyes to the overwhelming love inside her heart. "God has forgiven you, Nick. And so has your father. Isn't it about time you forgive yourself?"

He wiped the single tear from her face. "Isn't it about time we both forgive ourselves?"

He was right. She'd blamed herself for Sonny's misdeeds and his death. Nick had been through a similar pain. Maybe that was why God had brought them together.

"Let's forgive each other, right here, right now," she said, tears trailing down her face.

"Amen."

Together, they asked for God's forgiveness,

and together, they prayed for a new hope and a new beginning. Then they sealed it with a kiss.

And somewhere, high up in a tree, a gentle dove cooed softly, her sweet call echoing their prayer and lifting it up toward heaven.

"Momma, you look so pretty," Patrick said, a baseball glove in one hand and a Popsicle in the other.

Jesse nodded her agreement, her mouth opening with a squeal of glee. "It's the dress you dreamed about!"

Myla smiled down at her children. "Yes, it certainly is."

The green brocade dress brought back all the memories she'd stored up like a hidden treasure in her mind. It was a beautiful dress, but the real treasure was in the man who'd given it to her. Yet she'd chosen to leave him.

And he'd honored her choice by biding his time, learning patience, doing things that made her more and more proud of him each day.

He'd helped her realize her dream. She now had her own home. Glancing around the white walls of her small living room, Myla again felt the pride of being here, safe and in control, self-sufficient. That she'd gotten the house on her own merit helped to ease her loneliness. Maybe that should be enough.

But lately, other dreams had been filtering into her mind. What was stopping her from rushing into Nick's arms? What was holding her back from being with the man she loved with all her heart?

Knowing Nick had suffered a pain so similar to her own had made Myla see she'd been unfair to him right from the beginning. Nick was a self-made man, fashioned after his father's skewed idea of the perfect son. When he'd realized his father's stipulations were really a sham, that there was no foundation holding up his father's firm declarations, Nick had turned bitter. But Myla had seen that bitterness melt into a warmth that promised a new beginning for Nick. He was the best of his father, and his mother.

Tonight, she'd tell Nick that she loved him. She was out here on her own now, secure and confident that she could handle any situation. Although Nick had helped her along the way, she'd earned her catering reputation with her hard work and her determination, and she'd earned this house through her own efforts and the backing of a group dedicated to helping others. She wouldn't let any of them down.

Especially Nick.

Car lights illuminated the front yard, shining through the screen door like a spotlight. A neighbor's teenage daughter, a sweet girl named

Lily, came into the room with popcorn, all set to stay with the children and enjoy a movie on television.

"Looks like your date's here," Lily said, her expression dreamy. "Wow, he's nice-looking."

"Yes, he is," Myla had to agree.

"Isn't he the one that planted that big yellow rose out by the front steps?"

"The very one," Myla replied, remembering the morning she'd awakened to find the beautiful rose planted underneath her bedroom window. She'd fallen for him all over again.

Nick stepped onto the porch, his gaze settling on Myla as she opened the screen door. "You look great," he said, his eyes sweeping over her. "I'm as nervous as a teenager at his first prom."

"You don't look nervous," she said with a breathless laugh. "Black tie becomes you, Mr. Rudolph."

He tugged at his bow tie. "Thank you. Green brocade becomes you. Are you ready?"

"Ah…yes." She grabbed the small black purse she'd found at a secondhand store. Turning to the children, she said, "Behave for Lily, okay? And go to bed on time."

"I'll stay as long as you need me," Lily offered.

"Thanks," Myla said. She leaned down to kiss Patrick and then Jesse. "I love you," she whispered.

Her words tore through Nick. He wanted her to say those words to him. But he was fast losing hope. He'd watched her walk out of his home; he'd let her go, hoping against hope that she'd come back. He couldn't bear to have her out of his life, but he'd planted her a yellow rose as a symbol of her new freedom. When would she come back home to him?

He guided her down the steps, silent and serious, then helped her into the car, his heart now a hopeless mess, his mind tortured with loneliness.

Myla noticed his silence and tried to relax, but her nerves were strung tight. Thinking of how she'd changed since her first ride in this car, she looked out the window, watching the cottages and apartments give way to businesses and skyscrapers as they headed downtown to the Expo Hall located on the Red River.

"Are you all right?" Nick asked, his eyes on the road.

"Fine." She chanced a glance at him, wanting to ask him the same thing. "I just hope I don't embarrass myself or you."

"You won't. You probably gave the hardest speech of your life that night in my kitchen when you first told me about Sonny."

They reached the parking lot, which was already packed. Nick concentrated on finding a spot close to the building. Pulling the car into place, he switched off the ignition, then turned to Myla. "Before we go in, I just wanted to tell you—" With a groan, he reached for her, kissing her firmly on the lips. Then he let her go to stare at her. "Good luck."

"Thanks," she said, breathless. "I'll need a little luck to survive this speech." Especially after that kiss.

"Oh, you'll survive. That's what you do best."

Stopping him, she said, "Nick, I couldn't have survived these past few months, not without you."

She wanted to say more, but his continuing dark mood only added to her anxiety. Was he having doubts of his own?

As Nick helped her out of the car, then quietly and firmly guided her toward the doors of the big building, her heart sank. He seemed so distant tonight, more like the old Nick. Yet his kiss had been so real, so stirring. Maybe she was just imagining things because of her jittery nerves.

After the speech, then, she'd tell him she loved him. If it wasn't too late.

Inside, the glittering crowd of some of the city's richest patrons contrasted sharply with their purpose of being here. Lydia had estimated they'd be raising over one hundred thousand dollars to help build and remodel low-cost housing.

The minute they entered the massive hall, people began to stop Nick, shaking his hand, patting him on the back, congratulating him for being the steering force behind this ad hoc organization. He introduced Myla as they went along, but the glamorous faces started to merge in her mind.

Then the reporter who'd been in on the first committee meeting walked up to greet them. "Hello, Nick," Brooke Alexander said, her smile beaming as brightly as her simple diamond pendant.

Nick shook her hand. "Hi, Brooke, how are things at KTAS?"

"Great." Turning to Myla, the petite brunette said, "Good to see you again, Mrs. Howell. I understand you'll be giving testimony to HFL, Incorporated's good work here tonight."

Myla nodded. "Yes, as you know, I'm one of the recipients of that good work. The Rudolphs have helped me tremendously over the past few months."

Brooke stuck her microphone in Nick's face. "What do you have to say about that, Nick? You used to be called ruthless. You always wanted to remain anonymous, sort of a silent backer. Since serving on this undertaking with you, I've seen a different Nick Rudolph. Care to tell our viewers what's changed?"

Nick looked at the woman in green beside him, his eyes locking with hers. "A lot of things, but mostly, my attitude. Now, if you'll excuse us—"

With that, he urged Myla to keep moving. "I've had enough of reporters for one night."

Myla glanced back at him, thinking maybe she'd figured out the reason for his dark mood. "She's right, though, isn't she? You did want to remain anonymous before."

Nick shot her a frustrated look, tugging her close in the crowded room. "Yeah, right. Well, not anymore. I'm right here in the spotlight tonight, and involved in every aspect of this new organization."

Aggravated with his sarcasm, she said, "Well, why do you look so miserable?"

"Because I'd rather be somewhere else, alone with you." His eyes blazing, he said, "I miss you, Myla. I prayed for patience, but it isn't working."

She couldn't help her smile, and the wave of relief that washed over her. "I can tell."

"I want you back," he said just as the crowd shifted, pushing them together. He stared down at her, longing to tell her what was in his heart. But he'd promised to give her time. So he could only hold her close, taking in the fresh scent of her upswept hair, taking in the emerald green of her shining eyes as he fell in love with her all over again. "I want…to kiss you again."

Before Myla could tell him that she wanted to be back with him, and that she wanted him to kiss her again, Brooke Alexander appeared by his side. "Oh, Nick, I had one more question."

Groaning, Nick tried to be polite to the smug woman. "Look, Brooke, I don't have any comments to contribute to your newscast. I just want to enjoy this evening."

"Oh, don't be so modest," Brooke insisted. "Everyone knows you spearheaded this organization, but do they know the real story?"

"What story?" he asked warily, his gaze shifting from Myla to the jeering reporter.

The reporter leaned forward, her tone conspiring as she covered her mike. "From what my sources tell me, you had a lot more to do with Mrs. Howell getting this first house than anyone is aware of. Rumor has it your relationship with her involves more than just a neighborly concern."

Nick tried to pry Myla away, but she stood watching the reporter's face expectantly. The woman was obviously implying she knew about their relationship, Myla decided. Well, she wouldn't let Nick take the heat, and she certainly wouldn't let this woman turn their relationship into something other than what it was, just for the sake of sensationalism.

"It does involve more," she said, deciding honesty would be the best policy. She'd tell this nosy newshound the facts about what a good man Nick Rudolph really was. "It involves people caring about the community; it involves a kind, decent man helping someone in need. I think your viewers should know that, Brooke."

Sensing she had a story, Brooke Alexander pressed closer. "Anything else you'd like my viewers to know, Mrs. Howell?"

Nick tried to shove Myla away from the pesky woman. "No, she doesn't have anything else to say. As you know from serving on this committee, Mrs. Howell had to be approved by the *entire* board of directors in order to receive her house. I actually had very little to do with their decision to finance her house."

That didn't stop the reporter. "But shouldn't she know *who* donated the house she's living in?"

That stopped Myla in her tracks. "What do you mean?"

Her expression triumphant, Brooke continued, "We all know about the volunteers who've worked on remodeling the house, but we don't have the whole story on the person who actually gave the house to Hope, Faith and Love, Incorporated."

Shoving the mike back at Myla, she asked, "Wouldn't you like to know who that person is,

Mrs. Howell, so you could thank *him* personally and publicly?"

Myla's heart raced as fast as her mind. It didn't take much to figure out what the reporter was hinting at. Nick had bought her house for her. That's why this had been too easy. Why hadn't she seen it before? Maybe because she hadn't wanted to?

Before she could comment, Nick tugged her through the crowd. "Just keep walking."

"What was that all about?" she asked. "Or should I tell you? When he didn't turn around, she said, "You *gave* me that house, didn't you?"

Nick looked at her as if she'd gone daft, but she saw the truth in his eyes.

"You did. You bought me a house!" Anger spilling forth, she added, "After all that talk about the board's approval and other people being screened, you handpicked a house for me, then you just gave it to me. I didn't get it on my own, after all."

Dragging her close, Nick decided it was time to put all of his thoughts into action. "All right, yes! I bought the house—to remodel for you— because I love you."

That declaration stopped her. "Love? You love me?" Even as her heart swelled, she relived the dread that being married to Sonny had brought her. "But you deceived me, Nick. This is downright unethical, just like something Sonny would have pulled."

"I am *not* Sonny," he said, drawing a weary breath. "And for months now, I've been trying to prove that to you. I wanted you to be happy, Myla, and if that meant letting you go, then—"

"Happy?" She snapped the one word back at him. "How can I be happy knowing the man I love lied to me about something so important?"

Through his embarrassment, Nick saw a ray of hope. She'd said *the man I love*. He'd heard her, and so had half the city. He had witnesses.

All around them, people were staring and whispering, some with smiles on their faces, others with shock registered in their eyes.

"I wasn't deceitful," he insisted. "I didn't lie to you. I just never exactly spelled out the stipulations. All I did was buy a piece of run-down property. As a matter of fact, I bought several. Then I backed off and let the board decide the rest." Wanting to convince her, he said, "There were several applicants, too, but you had the best record. You had two jobs, and you were trying to find a place to live. A lot of the board members remembered you from our famous Christmas party, so they knew you were working on improving your situation.

"The other applicants, while needy, didn't seem as determined as you. One complained about having to work on the house, and the other, well, he took off to another state with some hefty donations he'd stolen from Magnolia House. I'm learning that not everyone is as trustworthy as you, Myla."

"So am I," she retorted, tapping her foot in agitation, her green eyes blazing fire.

"Just try to understand," he said lamely, wishing hard that he'd been honest with her all along. "I just wanted you to have a chance."

"*Everyone* who applied for that house deserved the same chance," she said, her anger calming to a slow boil. "But you bypassed that and gave the house to me."

"No, I did not," he said in defense of his actions. "I simply donated a house to the cause. The board picked you. And me, well…yes, I wanted to help you. I'd already cost you your place at Magnolia House, so I wanted you to have what you most desired."

"I won't live there, not knowing you practically gave it to me."

"I did not give it to you. You still have to pay off the loan," he reminded her, hoping to encourage her to be reasonable. When she kept heading for the door, he added, "I only did it because I love you, Myla. You see, I learned another lesson my father forgot to teach me—the one about having to let something go, in order to prove your love."

"You have a funny way of interpreting that," she said over her shoulder.

Determined, he called after her in a loud booming voice, "Myla, let's stop fighting. We love each other. I need you. And you need me."

Embarrassed and aware of their growing audience, she gave him a scathing look. "No, I don't."

Nick waved a hand in the air, scattering curious, elegantly dressed people left and right. "Yes, you do. I know it. You know it. And now, everyone in Shreveport knows it."

Looking across the room at him, she said, "And they also know that you're still as ruthless as ever. How could I have ever trusted you?"

"Because we love each other."

She ran out the door. Behind him, Nick heard someone clapping. The entire mob chimed in with a hearty round of applause. Turning, he saw Lydia and Grant watching him, along with everybody else in town.

"Bravo!" Lydia called out. "Glad you two finally saw the light. Now go after her. She's still got to make her speech!"

Growling at his sister's unsinkable optimism, he called back, "I think she just did!"

He caught up with her out on the steps facing the river, where a spring breeze teased at her billowing skirt. Inside, the Shreveport Symphony launched into Mozart, while Nick's head buzzed with adrenalin and aggravation.

"Leave me alone," Myla said, her hair whipping in the wind. "I need to think."

Groaning, he jabbed a hand toward her face. "Myla, think about this—buying the property was the only way I could get things started. Someone had to donate the first house to be renovated. I had the funds to do it, but I knew you'd never agree to me just handing it over to you."

"Yes, you knew!" She faced him squarely, her eyes blazing. "But you did it anyway. Can't you see, Nick, I've lived with deceit and lies and hypocrisy for so long, I just can't tolerate it, even for a good reason, even for someone I—"

"Someone you love?" Nick reached out, pulling a sprig of burnished hair away from her face. "It's scary, isn't it?"

Her eyes widened with wonder. "You're scared, too, right? You've practically told me how scared you are. But you shouldn't have lied to me, Nick. We're supposed to trust each other, remember?"

His heart soaring, he tugged her around. "Of course, I'm scared, and of course, I trust you. It's myself I couldn't trust. Why do you think it took me so long to tell you how I feel? I'm so used to taking action, I forgot to just tell you with words."

She thought about how he'd opened up to her, sitting there on the porch that day. "You told me about your father. Why didn't you tell me what you'd done with the house?"

He shrugged, then looked away, out at the churning waters of the Red River. "You wanted the house. I wanted you to be happy. I guess I'm still working on the part about putting things into God's hands. This wouldn't have backfired on me, if I'd only placed more trust in Him."

"And if I'd put more trust in you," she admitted. Searching his face, Myla took a long, shuddering breath to control her skittish emotions. "We've both been busy trying to control *my* life. I've been as bad as you, not willing to give an inch because I felt I had to show everyone I could do it."

Laughing softly, he urged her to him. "Myla, sweet Myla. I don't want to control you. I just want to spend the rest of my life with you. We can have fun working out the details."

But she still wasn't so sure. "What do you see in me?"

Cupping her face between his hands, Nick searched her eyes. "I'll tell you what I see. I see a strong, beautiful woman who's worked hard to bring herself up out of poverty. I see hope, faith, love…and my own salvation."

She started to cry, then—tears of joy, mixed

with tears of pain, as her heart let go of its pride. "Oh, Nick. You planted me a rosebush. That was the sweetest thing. You planted me a rosebush at a house you managed to get for me—just so you could give me the freedom to make my own choice. There is no greater sacrifice than that."

Loving her logic, Nick said, "I had to let you go, in order to win you back. It was the hardest thing I've ever tried to do. Please tell me I didn't fail completely."

Watching his face, seeing the sincerity and fear playing through his eyes, Myla was touched in that distant, secret spot where she'd stored up her love for him. Nick had the same doubts, had known the same pain and hopelessness she'd once known. But in spite of it all, he'd stood by her and her children. She realized with a burst of joy that neither of them had had a choice in the matter.

It had been in God's hands all along.

As if reading her thoughts, Nick said, "Myla, if I didn't have a dime to offer you, I'd still want to help you, to give you anything to make you happy and secure. I'd never desert you or try to control you. I just want to love you, to spend my life with you, whether it's at my house or yours. Wherever you are—that's my home, Myla. And that's the honest truth."

With that, Myla threw herself in his arms. "We both had something to prove."

Nick hugged her close, relief washing over him. He'd never make the same mistake twice. From here on out, he'd be completely honest with her, and with himself. Starting now.

Letting her go, he bent down on one knee. With the Red River flowing by a few feet away from them, he took her hand in his. "Now that we've settled all of that, I have something to ask you."

Myla's eyes widened while her heart fluttered like the flags flapping in the wind above their heads. "Yes?"

"Okay, I was only going to ask if I could have your cheesecake at dinner."

With both hands, she playfully slapped him on the shoulders. "Oh, you!"

Lifting his head, Nick asked her the real question on his mind. "Will you marry me?"

Tears fell down her cheeks. "Will you stop doing things behind my back in the name of love?"

"Hey, I'm doing the asking here, but yes, I promise to be completely up front with you—always. Now, I repeat, will you marry me?"

"Yes, I'll marry you."

"Do you love me?"

"I do love you."

"That's good, because I love you, too. Let's have pizza at the wedding reception. And a huge, fattening pound cake."

"Okay." She waited for him to stand, then threw herself into his arms for that other kiss they had both been wanting.

Nick enjoyed the kiss, then looked at his watch. "Come on, you have a speech to make."

"Wait." She reached into her clutch purse to pull out her dog-eared copy of the speech she'd prepared. "I don't need any pointers. I know exactly what I want to say."

"And what's that?"

Myla stopped, looking up at him, her eyes filled with tenderness. "I couldn't have done it without hope, faith, and…love."

Nick looked up at the stars twinkling over their heads. "And the greatest of these is love."

"That's right," Myla said, moving up the steps toward the ballroom. "It's all a matter of knowing whom to trust."

Epilogue

❧

"Quite a crowd today," Nick said, his arm wrapped around his wife's slender waist.

"Yes, but we expected that with the holidays so near." Leaning against him, Myla watched as people came and went, Christmas packages tucked underneath their arms, the smell of fresh-baked bread and homemade vegetable soup wafting around them.

"Well, you should be proud. I am." Nick kissed the top of her head, then patted the soft rounding bulge just beginning to show in her stomach. "We have a lot to be thankful for this Christmas."

"Uh-huh." Myla grimaced. "If I can just get through morning sickness."

"Feel bad?"

"No, I feel marvelous, happy and in the Christmas spirit. I can handle a little nausea."

"Yeah, I believe you can handle just about anything. Guess that's why I love you so much." He gave her another peck on the cheek, then let her go. "I've got to get moving. The next group of volunteers is waiting for me to teach them how to build houses. Come on, walk me to the truck."

Myla followed him through the glass double doors of the modest brick building, squinting at the noonday sun running down Line Avenue. After eight months of marriage, she was still very much in love.

And amazed at how blessed her life was now. She'd become partners with Grant, her soon-to-be brother-in-law. Then, keeping that partnership intact, and with Nick's encouragement, she'd opened up this place.

Bread of Life was more than a restaurant, though. It was a unique place where people who didn't have money for food could eat a good hot meal, along with some of the most influential people in the city, who paid donations to keep the nonprofit restaurant open. So far, the response had been tremendous.

Homeless people found hope here, in the form of job offers or assistance with education, or medical needs.

Nick liked to tell people it offered more than a meal, it offered solutions. And he was now a vital part of those solutions, a devout advocate for homeless rights and ways of getting people off the streets and back to productive lives.

He and Myla had even toned down their own lives, remodeling the mansion to make it more childproof and homey, and putting a needy family in the house he'd originally donated for Myla.

Reaching his used work truck where Jessica and Patrick sat waiting, Nick turned now, pulling Myla into the circle of his arms. "Don't work too hard, Mrs. Rudolph. We've got a lot to celebrate this year."

Myla nuzzled his neck, savoring the warmth and security he always offered. "Yes, we certainly do."

"Hey, Mama," Patrick called through the partially open window, "are you sure you're gonna be done here by Christmas?"

"Of course she will," Jessica replied in her proper, big-sister tone. "She's just doing her job first."

Giving her children that endearing look Nick loved so much, Myla nodded to her family. "I promise, I'll be home for Christmas."

Nick looked up to the shimmering winter sky, then smiled at his wife. "This year, we'll *all* be home for Christmas."

* * * * *

Dear Reader,

Homelessness has always been a problem the world over, yet we can never give up hope that it will eventually be solved.

This book has special meaning to me because I've worked with homeless people. I've visited homeless shelters and helped to feed people coming through a soup line. And the one thing I've noticed about homeless human beings is that they don't always know that someone cares about them. Sometimes, they just want to give up.

While Myla's story is part fairy tale and part reality, I know there are women out there who can achieve the same successes she achieves, and there are organizations willing to help these women every step of the way.

It's not easy, but there is a way to break the cycle. I hope my story will inspire some of you to work toward helping the homeless and, in doing so, find nourishment for your own soul.

Until next time, may angels watch over you while you sleep.

Lenora Worth

REQUEST YOUR FREE BOOKS!

2 FREE RIVETING INSPIRATIONAL NOVELS
PLUS 2 FREE MYSTERY GIFTS

Love Inspired®
SUSPENSE

YES! Please send me 2 FREE Love Inspired® Suspense novels and my 2 FREE mystery gifts (gifts are worth about $10). After receiving them, if I don't wish to receive any more books, I can return the shipping statement marked "cancel." If I don't cancel, I will receive 4 brand-new novels every month and be billed just $4.74 per book in the U.S. or $5.24 per book in Canada. That's a savings of at least 21% off the cover price. It's quite a bargain! Shipping and handling is just 50¢ per book in the U.S. and 75¢ per book in Canada.* I understand that accepting the 2 free books and gifts places me under no obligation to buy anything. I can always return a shipment and cancel at any time. Even if I never buy another book, the two free books and gifts are mine to keep forever.

123/323 IDN F5AN

Name	(PLEASE PRINT)	
Address		Apt. #
City	State/Prov.	Zip/Postal Code

Signature (if under 18, a parent or guardian must sign)

Mail to the **Harlequin® Reader Service:**
IN U.S.A.: P.O. Box 1867, Buffalo, NY 14240-1867
IN CANADA: P.O. Box 609, Fort Erie, Ontario L2A 5X3

**Are you a current subscriber to Love Inspired Suspense books
and want to receive the larger-print edition?**
Call 1-800-873-8635 or visit www.ReaderService.com.

* Terms and prices subject to change without notice. Prices do not include applicable taxes. Sales tax applicable in N.Y. Canadian residents will be charged applicable taxes. Offer not valid in Quebec. This offer is limited to one order per household. Not valid for current subscribers to Love Inspired Suspense books. All orders subject to credit approval. Credit or debit balances in a customer's account(s) may be offset by any other outstanding balance owed by or to the customer. Please allow 4 to 6 weeks for delivery. Offer available while quantities last.

Your Privacy—The Harlequin® Reader Service is committed to protecting your privacy. Our Privacy Policy is available online at www.ReaderService.com or upon request from the Harlequin Reader Service.
We make a portion of our mailing list available to reputable third parties that offer products we believe may interest you. If you prefer that we not exchange your name with third parties, or if you wish to clarify or modify your communication preferences, please visit us at www.ReaderService.com/consumerchoice or write to us at Harlequin Reader Service Preference Service, P.O. Box 9062, Buffalo, NY 14269. Include your complete name and address.

LISDIR13R

REQUEST YOUR FREE BOOKS!

2 FREE INSPIRATIONAL NOVELS
PLUS 2
FREE
MYSTERY GIFTS

Love Inspired
HISTORICAL
INSPIRATIONAL HISTORICAL ROMANCE

YES! Please send me 2 FREE Love Inspired® Historical novels and my 2 FREE mystery gifts (gifts are worth about $10). After receiving them, if I don't wish to receive any more books, I can return the shipping statement marked "cancel." If I don't cancel, I will receive 4 brand-new novels every month and be billed just $4.74 per book in the U.S. or $5.24 per book in Canada. That's a savings of at least 21% off the cover price. It's quite a bargain! Shipping and handling is just 50¢ per book in the U.S. and 75¢ per book in Canada.* I understand that accepting the 2 free books and gifts places me under no obligation to buy anything. I can always return a shipment and cancel at any time. Even if I never buy another book, the two free books and gifts are mine to keep forever.

102/302 IDN F5CY

Name	(PLEASE PRINT)	
Address		Apt. #
City	State/Prov.	Zip/Postal Code

Signature (if under 18, a parent or guardian must sign)

Mail to the Harlequin® Reader Service:
IN U.S.A.: P.O. Box 1867, Buffalo, NY 14240-1867
IN CANADA: P.O. Box 609, Fort Erie, Ontario L2A 5X3

Want to try two free books from another series?
Call 1-800-873-8635 or visit www.ReaderService.com.

* Terms and prices subject to change without notice. Prices do not include applicable taxes. Sales tax applicable in N.Y. Canadian residents will be charged applicable taxes. Offer not valid in Quebec. This offer is limited to one order per household. Not valid for current subscribers to Love Inspired Historical books. All orders subject to credit approval. Credit or debit balances in a customer's account(s) may be offset by any other outstanding balance owed by or to the customer. Please allow 4 to 6 weeks for delivery. Offer available while quantities last.

Your Privacy—The Harlequin® Reader Service is committed to protecting your privacy. Our Privacy Policy is available online at www.ReaderService.com or upon request from the Harlequin Reader Service.

We make a portion of our mailing list available to reputable third parties that offer products we believe may interest you. If you prefer that we not exchange your name with third parties, or if you wish to clarify or modify your communication preferences, please visit us at www.ReaderService.com/consumerschoice or write to us at Harlequin Reader Service Preference Service, P.O. Box 9062, Buffalo, NY 14269. Include your complete name and address.

LIHDIR13R